SUPERMODELS!

COLIN COSTELLO

120
pages

ISBN-10: 1-947197-06-1
ISBN-13: 978-1-947197-06-0

120pages
Subway Sites LLC
PO BOX 231548
New York, NY 10023

120pages.com

HOW TO READ A SCREENPLAY

A screenplay is written to show, not tell. Screenplays convey how a film will play out. The story unfolds through the dialogue and actions of the characters. As such, words are used economically. There is less description than you would find in a novel, as those details are typically handled during the production process. There is very little exposition; the screenplay doesn't provide any information that an audience watching the film wouldn't receive.

Therefore, as you read, visualize a film in your mind and "see" it as if you were watching a film.

If you're not familiar with the screenplay format, here are some things to know:

SCENE HEADINGS

Scene headings describe where the action takes place, the time of day, and sometimes additional details, such as if the action takes place in a flashback or as part of a montage.

For example:

```
INT. SAMMY'S HOUSE - DAY
```

"INT" indicates the action is indoors. "SAMMY'S HOUSE" tells us the action is in a woman's house. "DAY" tells us that it is daytime.

```
EXT. PARK - NIGHT
```

"EXT" indicates the action is outdoors. "PARK" tells us we are in a park. "NIGHT" tells us that it is the evening.

Other time descriptions may be used, such as "SAME" to indicate action taking place simultaneously or "LATER" to indicate action taking place moments later, after a brief jump in time.

CAPITALIZED WORDS

Throughout a screenplay, you may come across CAPITALIZED WORDS. These generally indicate the introduction of a new character, that the camera should pay attention to a particular item/sound/person/location, or that we are moving into a specific place within the location.

For example:

```
John turns.  He sees SALLY, the most beautiful girl he has ever
laid eyes on.  In her hands, she holds AN ADORABLE PUPPY.
```

DIALOGUE

Dialogue is written by centering a character's name with their spoken words appearing beneath their name. For example:

```
                    JOHN
          You found Charlie!
```

PARANTHETICALS

Between the character's name and dialogue, you may see text in parenthesis. This indicates some specific direction about how the dialogue is to be read or some specific action that takes place during the delivery of the dialogue.

```
                    JOHN
             (eyes watering)
          You found Charlie!
```

OTHER TERMS

Here are some other terms you may come across when reading a screenplay:

`(O.S.)` or `(O.C.)` – Off-screen or off-camera indicates that we do not see a character when dialogue is heard

`(V.O.)` – Indicates voiceover. This is dialogue we hear, but the speaker is not physically present in the same location as the action

`(CONT'D)` – Indicates that the same character is continuing to deliver a line of dialogue after an action, scene change, or page break

`(MORE)` – Indicates that the dialogue from the character continues on the next page

`POV` – Indicates that we see the action through a defined point of view

`SUPERIMPOSE` – Indicates that we see text on screen, often to define a time or location

`MONTAGE` – Indicates rapid cutting of different scenes in a sequence, such as any training sequence in a Rocky movie

`(beat)` – Indicates that a character takes a brief pause before continuing dialogue

To my real life super role models,
Chloe Pearl Costello and Maxine Rose Costello.

A BLACK SCREEN.

HEROIC MUSIC UP.

Blinding Camera flashes POP obliterate the blackness as the
title SUPERMODELS! barrels dramatically across... We focus on
the exclamation point and RACE in...

EXT. CITY SQUARE - NIGHT (ANGEL CITY)

Glass and steel... if Tokyo had babies with New York.

One neon billboard features four ridiculously hot models,
each posing seductively and holding a different product from
the Van Swoon Cosmetic Line - *Superheroine*. The slogan: "Be
Super."

WHOOSH!

A SMALL FLYING SAUCER SLAMS through the billboard... picks up
speed as it zeroes in on its target - The First Bank of Angel
City.

The saucer stops in mid-air and hovers.

Gears SPIN. Eight mechanical spider legs emerge.

A round steel platform lowers, revealing - a MASKED HISPANIC
VILLAINESS, 20, dressed in a skin tight body suit with spider
accents. SPIDRA.

She slinks off the platform; pirouettes to the bank doors.

Spidra lifts her stiletto heel, twists it off, releases the
other one and throws both.

The heels puncture the door. Rapid green, yellow and red
lights race up and down their sides. Stops on green.

BOOM!

Bank doors rocket outward. Alarms ring. A city bus flips
over. Two cars fly through the air... land on a fire hydrant,
causing it to shoot an arc of water.

Beaming at her destruction, she skips and twirls to the door.

                    SUPERHEROINE'S VOICE (O.C.)
          You've spun your last web
          of crime, Spidra!

Spidra turns. SUPERHEROINE ONE, 21, stands underneath the
billboard. She's masked, dressed in a skintight costume.

2.

Her thick blonde mane blows dramatically. *There's no way she should be fighting in this.*

                    SPIDRA
             (snickers; over the top)
          My poor misguided little fly,
          it's going to take more than
          you to stop me.

               SUPERHEROINE ONE
           (smirks; wooden delivery)
          I always accessorize. Count off.

SUPERHEROINE TWO, an African American, 19, masked, in a sexy costume and cape, springs to the a building's ledge. She carries a rocket skateboard.

               SUPERHEROINE TWO
      One.

SUPERHEROINE THREE, 19, gorgeous with curly black hair and major 'tude, stands on top of the overturned bus. She tugs her thigh high boot. Winces.

              SUPERHEROINE THREE
           (heavy Italian accent)
      Due.

              SUPERHEROINE ONE
      And I make three. Now, who feels
      like a big bag of suck?

              SPIDRA
      Once again I have a leg... oopsy--

Off their looks, a robotic spider leg emerges from behind her back, followed by seven more.

              SPIDRA
      -- make that eight legs up on you.

Spidra assumes a fighter's stance.

              SPIDRA
      And, girls, I brought party favors.

Hundreds of tiny robot spiders rush out of the saucer.

              SUPERHERO ONE
      Supermodels, work it!

Superheroine One points a rocket gun at the bank. A tether and hook bursts out, attaching itself to the gusset. She swings.

Superheroine Two jumps on her rocketboard. Take off!

Superheroine One narrows her eyes as she closes in on her target.

DRIP!

Blonde hair color mixes with sweat and drizzles down from her hair to her eyes, blinding her.

                    SUPERHEROINE ONE
          Cant see... Can't see!

Superheroine Two sees the collision that's about to happen... tries to avoid it... looks down; quickly glances at Superheroine Three's lipstick... which is smeared.

WHAM!

The two SMACK into each other and spin in the air. The rocketboard loses control and falls. Spidra runs.

Too late.

The villain loses her balance... trips over the board, knocking herself backwards. Spidra's legs SLAM into the bank columns, causing them to crumble.

BA-DOOM!

The columns crush the spiders...

Major disaster area. One and Two hang tangled mysteriously in the air. Three sighs; kicks off her boots and takes a smartphone out from her bra.

A god-like woman's voice *BOOMS* from the heavens.

                    WOMAN (O.S.)
          CUT!

A bell *RINGS*... lights go up.

SPIDRA coughs up dust. She takes off her mask, revealing purple-haired TANIA TABAREZ, a model from the billboard. She slowly rises, her spider legs attached to puppeteer's wire. She's discombobulated. And worse - her make-up's runny.

                    SPIDRA (TANIA)
               (dazed)
          Superheroine ... Save the Day. Save
          The Night.

She trips over a spider leg. CRACKS TWO NAILS -- LETS LOOSE.

                    SUPERHEROINE THREE
          Francesca's feet... my beautiful
          feet. Those boots!

FILM CREW GUYS rush and wrestle over ladders.

*REVEAL: It's not a city, but an elaborate commercial set.
Cars, on hydraulics, return to their original positions.*

Up in the air, hanging on harnesses against green screen, are
One and Two - models CHLOE CONNOR and MAXINE "MAX" MILES,
respectively. Chloe continues to drip. *Eww.*

                    CHLOE
          Excuse you.

                    MAX
          I know you're not blaming this on
          me, Chloe.

                    CHLOE
          Hmmm... let me think... Yes, I am.

                    MAX
          If your hair didn't look like Emma
          Stone's crackhead stylist curled it
          then you might have seen me coming.

On the bus, Three rips off her mask, revealing that she, too,
is a model on the billboard, FRANCESCA FOX. She talks into
her blue tooth headset as she climbs down the ladder.

                    FRANCESCA
          This lipstick is shit. Francesca,
          the greatest model from Milan, will
          not promote shit. I will not calm
          down. I want out of this contract.
               (her agent says something)
          Then I call Mafia!

Tania, studies her two broken nails. She turns to LOUD HEELS
CLICKING against steel catwalk stairs.

Out of the darkness emerges OLGA VAN SWOON, 49, powerful,
beautiful, conniving. Lex Luthor meet Cruella De Ville.
Standing next to her is assistant, TESA THOMPSON, 21,
efficient, mousy.

An anxious DIRECTOR moves to Olga, who assesses the disaster.

                    OLGA
          How long until we reset?

                    DIRECTOR
          They tell me hours.

Olga notices Tania's smeared make-up. Olga takes binoculars
from Tesa. She zooms in on the two hanging models who are
lowered. Their make-up is a wreck, too.

                    CHLOE
          Your skin cream stinks. Its fumes
          are making me stupid dizzy.

                    MAX
          That's the best you can come up?

                    CHLOE
          No. Nice tan, Max. Spray on or bed?

                    MAX
          I'm African American.

They reach the floor. Crew guys unstrap them from their
harnesses.

                    CHLOE
          Twitter war, friend!

                    MAX
          Chloe, we're not friends. We're not
          even "frenemies."

                    CHLOE
          Well, just so you know - if we were
          friends, we wouldn't be.

Max's eyebrows buckle.

                    MAX
          Love the hair color... exactly what
          shade of gray is that?

Chloe stops a CREW GUY.

                    CHLOE
          Mirror!

Olga turns to the Director; flashes a toothy smile.

                    OLGA
          At least the girls weren't injured. I
          think of them as my own daughters.

Tesa looks away. Olga spins on her heels.

                    OLGA
          Tesa, andale.

Olga walks to huge stage doors, now open. Tesa catches up.

                    OLGA
          I want a new director on
          set by lunch.

                    TESA
          Ms. Van Swoon, it's Friday.

Olga stops... turns... smiles...

                    OLGA
          I see.

Get me a new director or I'll rip your heart out.

                    TESA
          I'll make some calls.

                    OLGA
          Perfect, dahling.

Chloe chases after Olga.

                    CHLOE
          Ms. Van Swoon?

Olga turns. Flashes her toothy grin.

                    OLGA
          Yes, Chloe?

                    CHLOE
          Can't I work alone again? These
          girls...

                    OLGA
          Dear, we all have to learn to work
          together. New blood is always good.
          Keeps you on your toes. Helps you
          embrace who you are and who you're
          becoming.

Olga flashes a perfectly-capped grin, nods and walks to a
waiting black Van Swoon helicopter. It takes off.

INT. DRESSING ROOM - DAY

The girls sit in a row of director's chairs while MAKE-UP
TECHS "re-do" their faces. Tania studies her nails as the
Nail Tech applies polish.

She kisses one of them. Max puts a magazine face down.

> MAX
> You just need more folic acid.

She takes a sniff of Forever skin cream. *Whew! It does stink.*

> TANIA
> Girl, I don't drop acid.
> I just drink Tequila.

Chloe, towel around her head, talks to the Tech.

> CHLOE
> I want all this color out! Pronto!

Max tosses her costume from earlier.

> MAX
> No superhero would be caught dead
> wearing this. 100% impractical.

Chloe holds her hair up for the stylist.

> CHLOE
> Did you see what Superheroine did
> to my hair!?! This is an E-m-a-r-j-
> ancy!

Max turns.

> MAX
> I can't believe millions
> of girls look up to you.

Chloe smirks.

> CHLOE
> I've been on the cover of Cosmo
> twenty times in two years. What
> have you done? Role Model.

> MAX
> I spent my senior year
> volunteering for Unicef.

A flying lip gloss gets stuck in Chloe's thick hair.

> FRANCESCA (O.S.)
> Idiot! You are not fit to milk a
> cow!

> CHLOE
> Ow, Francesca! Don't get all Naomi!

A livid Francesca berates her Make-up Tech.

> FRANCESCA
> No one touches Francesca's mouth!
> Francesca's smile is worth millions!

A distressed Tesa enters.

> TESA
> That's a wrap. Can't find another
> director.

The four models look up.

> FRANCESCA
> Grazie a Dio.

She makes the sign of the cross. Chloe rips the towel off her head. Tesa works up the nerve...

> TESA
> Blendeds, anyone? I'm buying.

Francesca walks by, throws her towel on Tesa's shoulder as if she were the water boy.

> TESA
> You know - do a little girl-on-girl
> action. I-I-I mean bonding. We all
> need bonding.

Max stops. Shifts.

> MAX
> I... um... can't. I have to read up
> for...
> (whisper)
> ... a lecture.

> TANIA
> A lecture!?! Good one, girl.

Max and Tania hand their towels to Tesa. Chloe stops.

> CHLOE
> I'll go, Tesa.

                    TESA
          Really?

Chloe nods, brings out her Smartphone. Searches...

                    CHLOE
          For sure! Ooo can't today. I have a
          callback. Tomorrow... we have the
          Superheroine launch party. Oh Emm
          Gee I have to speak with my
          stylist. I have no idea what I'm
          going to wear. I have to run.

                    TESA
          Maybe some other time, Chloe!

Chloe hands Tesa her towel, then leaves. Tesa frowns.

INT/EXT. VAN SWOON LABS - R&D - DAY (AFTERNOON)

Somewhere in the desert. A large white futuristic facility
stands ominously.

A black helicopter, with the Van Swoon logo, lands on a
helipad. Olga's helped out by armed SECURITY GUARDS.

                    OLGA (OVER)
          You said Superheroine would last
          for one week! No matter what.

This is obviously more than just a lab for cosmetics. DR.
HUGO FANTANBURGER, 50s, short, meek, brilliant but crazed,
flinches at a livid Olga.

                    OLGA
          The nanobots didn't bond to the
          models' molecular structure.

                    DR. FANTANBURGER
               (stutters)
          There's an explanation, Ms. Van
          Swoon.

He taps buttons on a console. On a screen above him the
words: DIAGNOSTIC, INTELLIGENT, VIDEO, AUTOMATON appear. Dr.
Fantanburger punches an activate button.

Olga steps back, caught off guard, as a LARGE THREE-
DIMENSIONAL NON-DESCRIPT FACE made out of grids floats in the
center of the lab.

                    COMPUTER
                (*soothing voice*)
          Good afternoon, Dr. Fantanburger.

Olga raises an eyebrow.

                    DR. FANTANBURGER
          Uh, yes, good morning, Computer.

                    COMPUTER
          How may I be of service?

                    DR. FANTANBURGER
          Explain to Ms. Van Swoon, the
          concerns about The Superheroine
          Cosmetics line, please.

The head morphs into floating equations which morph into
other diagrams.

                    COMPUTER
          As nanobots move through matter,
          they interact with other charged
          particles, such as electrons--

Olga smirks at the explanation, holds up a hand.

                    OLGA
          I am not in need of a high school
          science lesson. I would simply like
          to know why my cosmetic line, which
          once withstood temperatures of two
          thousand degrees, is now utterly
          worthless?

The computer stares at Olga, then continues. Four nondescript
female figures float. Alpha rays pulse through their veins.

                    COMPUTER
          At low levels, the Alpha Radiation
          carried by the nanobots is not
          hazardous to the participants' DNA.
          However, if levels were increased,
          exposure to their living tissue
          could become severe and possibly
          catastrophic. Not only physically,
          but mentally.

Olga smiles...

                    OLGA
          So you lowered the concentration.

Dr. Fantanburger gulps, nods slowly.

                    DR. FANTANBURGER
          For their safety.

                    OLGA
          That's what waivers are for.

                    DR. FANTANBURGER
          Please. We need more time to assess
          the long term affects of
          Superheroine. The FDA would never
          approve.

Olga smiles and walks over to four outlandish costumes
hanging on a rack.

                    OLGA
          You have only one approval to worry
          about and it's not the FDA's I
          assure you.

                    DR. FANTANBURGER
          But if--

                    OLGA
          -- Hugo, I transferred you from
          Division 706 for your creativity,
          ingenuity and results track record.
          That is what I pay for. And all the
          shareholders care about.

Olga stares at the floating numbers and the outline of the
four models. She leaves. Over loud CLICKING HEELS...

                    OLGA
          Superheroine has been sold as the
          longest lasting cosmetic line ever
          put on God's green Earth. Better
          than permanent eyebrows. And
          tomorrow night we prove it to the
          world at the launch party.

Her eyes narrow.

INT/EXT. STAGE - DAY (AFTERNOON)

The models stop at the exit door. Adjust themselves and
jockey for position. Max quickly shoves her magazine into her
purse. Chloe muscles Francesca aside. Francesca pushes back.
Tania joins in the shoving.

Chloe throws the door open.

                    CHLOE
          You know what? We would make
          really good friends... Said no one
          ever.

The girls immediately change personas. Hordes of paparazzi
take their pics. The girls wave. SHOUTS of "Chloe! Francesca!
Max! Tania!" "Smile!"

A photographer, SAM BLAKE, 23, aims his camera at Chloe.

                    SAM
          Chloe... Over... here!

Chloe turns dramatically; makes eye contact with Sam. He
smiles bigger... she smiles back... Amazingly she walks to
him. Sam's mouth drops...

WHAM!

He's *"cock-blocked"* by a much taller and better looking
EUROPEAN PHOTOGRAPHER, 30s. NIGEL.

Chloe pulls Nigel by his camera strap and kisses him.

                    CHLOE
          Let's get out of here, baby.

EXT. BEACH - DAY (LATE AFTERNOON)

Chloe sits on the hood of a red Ferrari, looking at a mirror.
She runs a hand through her hair. Her eyes widen at a lone
gray hair.

                    CHLOE
          Oh Emm Gee, Max's right. Gray hair.
          My career's over.

Nigel changes a lens on his camera.

                    CHLOE
          Nigel, are you listening to me? I'm
          having an "ARP" moment.

He looks up, speaking in that Euro-trash accent that's
instantly despised. Aims his camera at Chloe.

                    NIGEL
          You are only 21, peach.

Nigel clicks off pics of her. She brings out a tweezer.

> CHLOE
> Twenty-one is 70 in model years. If
> anyone gets the idea that I'm on a
> one-way flight to *Jurassic Park*
> I'll never do another launch. My
> god no more Paris. No more fashion
> week.

She parts her hair, searching...

> NIGEL
> That's what air brushing is for.

> CHLOE
> What do old models do anyway? Oh, I
> know they disappear. Or appear on
> *Dancing with the Stars*. I can't
> dance.

Nigel ignores her, still taking shots.

> NIGEL
> Your insecurity is sexy.
> Animalistic. Smile for me.

Chloe smiles for the camera. Then finds a gray hair.

> CHLOE
> Another one?! I can't even...

INT/EXT. MAX'S HOUSE - DAY (LATE AFTERNOON)

Amazing. Very Orange County.

> MAX (O.S.)
> Mother, stop!

> DRUSILLA (O.S.)
> You are not leaving this house
> looking like that.

INT. MAX'S HOUSE - BEDROOM - CONTINUOUS

More library than a model's bedroom.

> MAX
> You're hurting me!

Max's MOTHER - DRUSILLA, 40s, is an older and more tricked
out version of Max - fake boobs, nails etc. She tries to
squeeze a pimple on Max's cheek.

                         DRUSILLA
               It's a red carpet event. Wonderful
               for <u>our</u> career. It's no use. We'll
               have to use concealer. Even though
               I don't know what would ever make
               that asteroid disappear.

Max storms around the room.

                         MAX
               You're stressing me! How could you
               make plans for me? With him...

She holds up a cover of A HIP-HOP MAGAZINE. Rapper CRAZY
EIGHT smiles on the cover.

                         DRUSILLA
               He's available and he will get us
               the PR we sorely need. I've also
               invited Mr. Crazy Eight to your
               launch tomorrow night. So you can
               stop once and for all with this
               nonsense.

She snatches Max's magazine out of her purse. It's *Science
Today*. On the cover is Dr. Fantanburger.

                         MAX
               What's wrong with bettering myself?
               I can't be a model forever. Look at
               the women in *Hidden Figures*!

                         DRUSILLA
               I did. That's why they were hidden.
               I forbid you to read anything other
               than *Elle* and *Paris Vogue*. Maybe *US
               Weekly*. Capiche!?! You will be the
               next Kim Kardashian.

Max frowns. Drusilla takes her magazine. Glances at the
headline - something about Alpha Particles.

                         DRUSILLA
               Now, unless these Alpha Particles
               can remove that horrid growth, he's
               of no use to us. Mr. Crazy Eight
               will be here in 10 minutes. Get on
               Twitter and tweet something witty.
               Or as I like to say, "twitty!"

                         MAX
                    (bummed)
               I was going to hear Dr.
               Fantanburger speak tonight.

Drusilla, ignoring her, sashays out of the room.

>   DRUSILLA (O.C.)
>   And don't you dare wear underwear.
>   Papparazzi will be out and about!

Max storms out of her room, past Drusilla...

EXT. MAX'S STREET - CONTINUOUS

Max turns just as CRAZY EIGHT'S limo arrives. Wearing a gold crown, he leans out of the window.

>   CRAZY EIGHT
>   What's crack-a-lacking, queen!?!

Horrified, Max runs up the block. She crosses the street, not looking.

SCREECH!

A Bentley convertible almost hits her. Max, slams her fists on the hood. Tania lifts her sunglasses. She looks at a nail. *Chipped.* The two glare at each other...

EXT. VAN SWOON CONSTRUCTION SITE - DUSK

Steel beams reach to the sky, only stopping at an uncompleted floor. From the top...

>   OLGA (O.S.)
>   As you can see...

ON THE TOP FLOOR, Olga addresses a group of UNIMPRESSED SHAREHOLDERS.

>   OLGA
>   ... we are completely on schedule.
>   The new Van Swoon Towers will be
>   the triumph of Angel City!

CLAP! CLAP!

Olga is the lone clapper. She stops, looks at their dour expressions. Off her look, STEWART, 50s, steps forward.

>   STEWART
>   We heard about the commercial.

Silence. Olga manages a smile.

                         OLGA
               A hiccup, Stewart.

A SECOND SHAREHOLDER, MARSHALL, 50s, joins in.

                         MARSHALL
               And we haven't seen one iota of
               proof that *Superheroine* is what you
               say it is.

Olga's face says, "reassurance and comfort." Her tightly
clenched fist behind her back says otherwise.

                         OLGA
               I realize the stock has seen better
               days. But like the phoenix, we will
               rise again -- beginning tomorrow
               night when *Superheroine* launches.

The shareholders don't seem convinced. Stewart sighs.

                         STEWART
               There is also chatter.

                         OLGA
               People will talk. I believe the
               younger set calls it, "jelly."

                         MARSHALL
               Of global dealings you've made on
               behalf of Van Swoon without our
               approval. This is unacceptable.

Olga pauses... smiles.

INT/EXT. TANIA'S CONVERTIBLE - TRAVELING - NIGHT

Tania zips in and out of traffic. Max holds on for dear life.

                         TANIA
               So tell your mom you want to quit.

                         MAX
               It'd be easier to enter rehab.

                         TANIA
               I know a good place in Utah. They
               have a righteous avocado bath.

Max throws her a look: *yeah right*. They stop.

                    TANIA
          We're here. Wait?
          You really did have a lecture? Do
          they serve alcohol?

Max turns... frowns. They've stopped in front of an
auditorium at Angel City University. The lights are off. The
poster announcing Fantanburger's speaking engagement has a
big red canceled label laid diagonally across it.

INT. TESA'S APARTMENT - BEDROOM - NIGHT

Tiny. Posters of Chloe, Max, Francesca and Tania cover walls.
Magazines, with them on the covers, blanket Tesa's bed. Loud
runway music blares. A framed certificate from Angel City
Modeling School hangs proudly.

Tesa, glasses off and hair down and is quite pretty, pretends
to walk down a runway in front of a full-length mirror.

                    TESA
          Ladies and gentlemen, wearing Van
          Swoon's newest cosmetic line,
          supermodel Tesa Thompson!

Tesa twirls in front the mirror, making ridiculous faces. She
looks at the certificate, then the models. Sighs.

                    TESA
          One day.

Her cell rings, throwing her off her game. She answers.

                    TESA
               (enraged)
          What!?!
               (returns to Tesa)
          Oh, hello, Ms. Van Swoon.

INT/EXT. HELICOPTER - TRAVELING - SAME TIME

Olga looks out over Angel City.

                    OLGA
          Tesa, I want the girls in hair and
          make-up at 6 AM.

Tesa looks at the clock. It's almost midnight.

                    TESA
          Ms. Van Swoon, it's almost
          midnight.

Olga's eyes flutter with annoyance.

> OLGA
>
> I see.

Deafening silence. Tesa gives in.

> TESA
>
> I'll let them know.

Olga smiles and hangs up. Olga punches in another number on her phone. After a few seconds, Dr. Fantanburger's face fills her screen.

> OLGA
>
> Hugo, do you have an update?

> DR. FANTANBURGER
>
> I managed to engineer a hair coloring solution, concealer, nail polish and a lipstick.

> OLGA
>
> Well, we'll have to make due won't we? And, Hugo, this time I want the cosmetics applied with The Transapplicator.

> DR. FANTANBURGER
>
> But it hasn't been tested.

> OLGA
>
> It will be tomorrow morning.

Olga hangs up. The helicopter continues on.

EXT. ANGEL CITY PARK - DAY (EARLY MORNING)

Empty. All is set up for the *Superheroine* launch party. Chloe shuffles across the lawn to a tent, yawning.

> MAX
>
> Good morning, Chloe!

Chloe turns. Groans. Max and Tania are wide awake.

> CHLOE
>
> Why are you two so disgustingly awake?

> TANIA
>
> I thought senior citizens always wake up early.

Chloe sneers.

                    MAX
          Need a walker, dear?

The three turn as Francesca, still in party clothes, gets out
of a cab and stumbles. She curses in Italian.

                    FRANCESCA
          Credo che diventerò pazzo!

The other three look at her, dumbfounded.

                    FRANCESCA
          Van Swoon has lost her mind! 6 AM!
          I hate each of you for it!

Tesa stops them.

                    TESA
          This way.

INT/EXT. HIGH-TECH TRAILER - CONTINUOUS

A long white moving lab. Sterile. High-tech.

                    OLGA (O.S.)
          Today, the four of you will become
          legends to women around the world.
          I envy you.

                    TANIA (O.S.)
          I've never seen make-up chairs like
          this.

THE GIRLS, in medical gowns, stand in a room full of computer
banks. LAB TECHNICIANS buzz about. Ahead, are four life-size
high-tech female molds, with high-tech clamps at the wrists
and ankles.

FACING THE MOLDS, IS A LARGE SATELLITE DISH-LIKE CONTRAPTION -
- THE TRANSAPPLICATOR.

                    TESA
          I could take Tania's--

                    OLGA
          -- Don't be ridiculous.

Dr. Fantanburger enters. A TECH brings him a metallic
cannister, marked, "eyeliner." He shakes his head.

                    DR. FANTANBURGER
          Much too unstable.

Max recognizes and runs to him.

                    MAX
          Dr. Fantanburger! I've read all of
          your books on Alpha Particles.

Francesca turns to Chloe. Sneers.

                    FRANCESCA
          It reads?

Chloe shrugs. Max invades Dr. Fantanburger's space.

                    MAX
          I went to your lecture last night.
          Why did you cancel?

Fantanburger looks over at Olga, then back at Max.

                    DR. FANTANBURGER
          I... uh... had a prior engagement.

Olga rushes over, coming in between the two.

                    OLGA
          Let's proceed shall we?

Fantanburger nods. Chloe moves forward. Tania stops her.

                    TANIA
          This doesn't feel right.

Chloe looks around.

                    CHLOE
          What?

                    TANIA
          Look around. Have you ever had make-
          up applied in anything remotely
          like this?

Chloe studies the situation. Looks over at Olga.

                    CHLOE
          Ms. Van Swoon?

                    OLGA
          Yes, dear?

                    CHLOE
          Superheroine doesn't contain any
          animal by-products does it?

Silence. Olga finally smiles.

                    OLGA
          No, I can honestly say it doesn't
          contain that.

Chloe smiles. Turns to Tania.

                    CHLOE
          Yaaaaas.

Bubbly, she skips to the molds. Clamps WHIR into place.
Fantanburger looks anxiously at Olga. Techs study readouts.
Tesa watches intensely. The Transapplicator glides in front
of them.

Max frowns.

                    MAX
          What is that?

                    DR. FANTANBURGER
               *(looks up from a
               clipboard)*
          The Transapplicator.

Olga steps in... flashes her toothy grin.

                    OLGA
          Just a new applications system
          patented solely by Van Swoon. This
          is Providence.

Dr. Fantanburger pushes buttons. Techs attach cables and
wires to other metal cannisters - each with a name. Nail
polish for T. Tabarez... hair color for C. Connor...
concealer for Max's and lipstick for Francesca.

Fantanburger puts on goggles; walks to Olga.

                    DR. FANTANBURGER
          We're ready.

Olga smiles, then snaps her fingers for Tesa and they leave.
Electro-mag locks seal the models in.

OBSERVATION ROOM - SAME TIME

Dr. Fantanburger nods at the Techs. Buttons are pushed on a control console. The room goes dark. Lights flash. Energy travels from the cannisters along the cables to the Transapplicator. It sizzles with blue electricity

The beams BLAST the girls.

-- NANOBOTS rush deep into Chloe's hair cells. Her hair and brain flash pink. A red streak forms in the center of her hair.

-- The cells in Tania's nails change size. And replicate rapidly. Her nails turn a perfect shade of red.

-- Max's cells alter in size and shape... some disappear.

-- Francesca's mouth turns various colors. The inside looks as if it is heating up. Her lips become ruby red and her teeth turn ultra-white.

Lights flicker back on. The girls look like they've been through a wind-tunnel. Olga rushes in along with Fantanburger, who takes off his goggles. Chloe breathes heavily.

> CHLOE
> I feel rejuvenated.

> DR. FANTANBURGER
> Check their vitals. Quickly.

Techs assess them. They each give the thumb's up sign. Olga leaves.

INT. DRESSING ROOM - LATER

House music BLARES. The excited models dress. Chloe stares at her new red streak. She smiles.

> CHLOE
> (sotto)
> Not a gray hair. Bring on the
> paparazzi.

Max touches where her pimple was. Concealed. As an assistant helps Tania into an outrageous dress, she looks at her reflection in her shiny nails.

Tesa runs in.

                    TESA
          Five minutes!

They file out. Tesa, excited, stops Francesca.

                    TESA
          Francesca, want to see my new tat?

Tesa lifts the back of her shirt. A snake. Francesca rolls
her eyes... touches her throat.

                    FRANCESCA
               (dry)
          Acqua!

                    TESA
          What?

                    FRANCESCA
          Water, you beast. Enough of this
          Francesca crush. You will never be
          one of us.

Tesa's crushed. Francesca snatches the water and walks on.
She guzzles the water, slams the bottle down. It's steaming
and melted...

EXT. STAGE - MOMENTS LATER

Packed. Loud music. Reporters, models, entertainment people
are everywhere.

Olga straightens herself, looks and saunters out onto the
stage. She stands at the microphone.

                    OLGA
          Thank you. Tonight, I give you, the
          world, my gift - the longest
          lasting cosmetic line ever created.
          I present *Superheroine*.

Lights go down. House music up.

BOOM!

Fireworks explode. Lights go up. Chloe, hair blowing, struts
onto the stage, She poses, winks at Nigel, spins.

ON SAM:

Sam is there again, muscling to get shots of Chloe. Nigel
blocks him.

24.

ON TESA:

Tesa grows angrier as she watches from behind stage.

ON MAX:

Max, in a bathing suit, struts out.

ON FRANCESCA:

Francesca follows, finally smiling, showing perfect white
teeth.

ON TANIA:

Tania walks onto the runway, flashing her nails. Olga nods at
the Van Swoon board, who show signs of smiling.

> OLGA
> Sun, sweat, rain, heat –
> *Superheroine* is impervious to all
> the elements. But don't take my
> word for it...

Rain pours on stage. Chloe's hair remains the same. The girls
lift their faces, then turn back to the audience. They're the
same. The crowd's amazed. Olga smiles at the shareholders,
who smile back.

Chloe suddenly STUMBLES. Her hair begins to sway.

Francesca grips her stomach and her mouth.

Max looks down at her foot... it fades away... then
reappears. Tania trips over herself as well. She grabs her
hand, amazed how her nails are glowing.

Concern rushes over Sam's face as he lowers his camera.

Fantanburger runs to the girls.

The girls grow sicker. Olga growls at Tesa.

> OLGA
> Close the curtain.

Tesa runs off. The shareholders storm away. Olga stares
ahead. Ruined.

INT/EXT. HIGH-TECH TRAILER - LATE NIGHT

Empty. Tesa, a mixture of emotions, studies The
Transapplicator. Turns on a switch. It hums to life.

                    TESA
          Ten years of modeling classes...

She positions the cannisters... pushes buttons. She spots the
eyeliner cannister and attaches it.

                    TESA
          Five thousand dollars on head
          shots...

She straps herself into Cindy's mold...

                    TESA
          ... too short... muffin top... not
          pretty enough...

Tesa lifts a remote control with her teeth, aims it.

                    TESA
          I'm just as good as any of you. In
          fact, I'm better!

She presses the remote. The Transapplicator bathes Tesa in
the Alpha Rays. She tries to shut off the remote but can't.
She panics. The snake tattoo glows. The remote drops out of
her mouth as more and more nanobots seep into her...

Tesa SCREAMS (O.S.). The door of the trailer blows off, flies
into the air--

                                        SLAM TO BLACK.

FADE IN:

INT. CHLOE'S CONDO - BEDROOM - DAY (EARLY MORNING)

Ultra-modern. A shrine to Chloe. Floor to ceiling framed
pictures of herself. Chloe lies, face down, on a platform
bed. A pillow covers her head.

The cell RINGS... RINGS... RINGS...

Through an open door, Nigel yells:

                    NIGEL (O.S.)
          Peach!

                    CHLOE
               (muffled)
          No interviews.

The cell stops. The pillow depresses in the middle as Chloe
sighs.

Nigel, shirtless and in pajama bottoms, rushes into the room and shoves her cell under the pillow. It rings again. She frowns.

CLOSE-UP: CELL SCREEN. "ANGEL CITY HERALD"

                                        CUT TO:

INT. DAILY HERALD - NOELLE HARDY'S DESK - SAME TIME

NOELLE HARDY is in her 20s, pretty, African American and very cool. Lois Lane meet Bob Woodward. She sits with her phone cradled between her shoulder and ear. It goes to Chloe's voicemail. Noelle hangs up.

                                    CUT BACK TO:

INT. CHLOE'S CONDO - BEDROOM - DAY (EARLY MORNING)

She sits on the edge of her bed.

We see that her red streak has been replaced by a white one. She slowly rises out of bed... shuffles past a full-length mirror.

Pauses. Blinks. Chloe's hand reaches up to her new white streak. Lifts a couple of white strands.

SCREAMS.

EXT. CITY STREET - DAY (MORNING)

Nigel and Chloe, in baseball cap and sunglasses, hurry.

                    NIGEL
          Enrique is the best hair dresser in
          town. He'll fix this in no time,
          Peach.

                    CHLOE
          Stop calling me, "peach." I'm not
          feeling like any kind of fruit
          right now.

They stop in front of a salon - *Follicle*. Chloe rushes in, letting the door SLAM on Nigel.

INT. FOLLICLE - MOMENTS LATER

Beverly Hills-esque. Chloe, still wearing her baseball cap
and now a black smock, sits in an uber-stylish chair.

ENRIQUE, very formidable, saunters out.

> CHLOE
> It's h-i-d-y-ous. Brace yourself.

> ENRIQUE
> B-r-r-r-racing.

Chloe lifts her sunglasses. Nigel joins the two. She takes
off her baseball cap. Their eyes widen. Chloe's hair has now
turned completely white. And her locks are way longer... down
to the middle of her back.

> ENRIQUE
> Gasp.

Chloe's lower lip trembles. Enrique lays a hand on her
shoulder.

> ENRIQUE
> Just because you look like you've
> seen the return of white socks and
> stilettoes doesn't mean I can't fix
> this. We just need new color. But
> I'll start by trimming some of your
> ends. Well all of them.

Enrique picks up scissors, then some of Chloe's hair. The
scissors open... he goes to cut--

FWOOSH!

Chloe's hair straightens and bats the scissors away. They
slide across the floor.

Silence. *Did that just really happen?*

> ENRIQUE
> If you thought I was taking too
> much off you could've just said so.

> CHLOE
> I didn't do anything, Enrique.

Silence again. Nigel picks up the scissors and hands them
back to Enrique. He moves to cut again. This time he cuts ONE
STRAND.

At lightening speed, a portion of Chloe's hair grabs the scissors and rockets them across the room, puncturing a wall. Another portion of her hair extends like Rapunzel and wraps itself around Enrique and throws him through a back door, splitting it in half.

Chloe, stunned and scared, bolts out of her chair.

> CHLOE
> Enrique!

She rips her smock off. Turns and looks in the mirror.

FWAM!

Sections of her hair rocket out in all directions. Some pick up a brush... others comb... another section turns on the faucet over the sink to wash itself. One portion adjusts Chloe's bra. And another turns on the radio and begins dancing.

Chloe processes. Then screams!

EXT. FOLLICLE - CONTINUOUS

Nigel, white as a ghost, bolts. Chloe's hair quickly return to its normal length as she runs out the door. Nigel's nowhere to be seen.

> CHLOE
> Nigel, wait!

INT/EXT. SMALL AIRPORT HANGER - MORNING

Olga's stretch limo comes to a stop. Olga, who hasn't had much sleep, steps out.

A LARGE BODYGUARD TYPE, 20s, suit dark glasses, opens her door. Olga doesn't say a word as they walk quickly to the hanger.

> OLGA
> Who else knows?

> BODYGUARD
> Just you.

Olga stops, turns...

> OLGA
> What about?

>BODYGUARD
>The Transapplicator wasn't damaged.

Olga relaxes. The two enter. OLGA'S TEAM paces.

>OLGA
>Find Tesa. Find her now.

She stands in front of what used to be the rolling laboratory. It's unrecognizable. Olga's cell rings. She takes it out of her purse... looks at the Caller ID. She's not thrilled. She answers.

>OLGA
>Yes? Yes, I'll be there shortly.

INT. DAILY HERALD - MR. BLAKE'S OFFICE - CONTINUOUS

Mr. Blake, 50s, portly, graying, basically Perry White and J. Jonah, stands by the window squeezing a continuous stream of drops into his eyes.

>SAM
>You know you're only supposed to
>use two drops at a time.

Sam notices Noelle typing at her desk. Mr. Blake puts the bottle down and walks to his desk. He blinks rapidly.

>SAM
>Did you see my photos from the
>launch last night? I nailed those
>models.

Mr. Blake sits down, sifts through Sam's photos.

>MR. BLAKE
>I'm overcome.

Sam smiles eagerly.

>MR. BLAKE
>I'm overcome because I have three
>ounces of Visine in my eyes and I
>can still see these are crap!

>SAM
>Dad?

                    MR. BLAKE
          Don't call me that. I can't believe
          your mother - god rest her soul -
          and I sank all that money into art
          school. Did you ever leave the frat
          to study?

He shoves Sam's photos across his desk. They spill to the
floor. They're horrible. Shots are blurry, blocked, over
exposed. Mr. Blake rubs his head.

                    SAM
          Dad, I can explain--

                    MR. BLAKE
          -- No allow me. This isn't your
          college paper where you can get
          away with murder because you're
          foolin' around with some sweater-
          wearing co-ed. I'm not wearing a
          sweater. This is a real newspaper
          with real stories. A newspaper that
          is quickly going out of business. I
          would've fired any other
          photographer for bringing me shots
          like this long ago. We're not
          running fake news here.

Sam picks up the photos, approaches the desk.

                    SAM
          Dad, I need something real. Real
          news you know? Not this Reddit
          crap. Something I can sink my teeth
          into.

Mr. Blake throws his hands up.

                    MR. BLAKE
          This <u>was</u> something real! When
          things blow up in Olga Van Swoon's
          face, that's news. Especially if
          all four of her models fall off the
          stage like they took mushrooms from
          the craft service table. Was it the
          competition? An inside job? A bad
          knish? That's news. And you blew
          it.

                    SAM
          Dad, give me another shot.

He walks over to the window.

> SAM
> I've got a nose for news. I'll
> prove it to you.

Sam looks out and down into...

EXT. ALLEY - MORNING

BLACK SCREEN:

TESA'S POV: The alley slowly comes into focus. A cat purrs.

> TESA (O.S.)
> *(gravely voice)*
> Here, kitty kitty...

The cat turns toward Tesa. Its hair raises and tail puffs out. And HISSES.

A GREEN LASER BEAM fires from Tesa's eyes. Tesa SCREAMS. She runs down the alley, tripping over garbage cans.

The cat has been petrified.

INT. COFFEE SHOP - DAY (LATE MORNING)

Chloe, back to wearing the cap and sunglasses, sits in a corner. She has a water and one cracker. She reads her cell.

CLOSE-UP: Cell Screen. The front page of The Herald: "COSMETIC LAUNCH GROUNDED" by Noelle Hardy.

She types on her phone.

CLOSE-UP: "I need you. I'm all alone."

She waits for an answer. There is none.

She puts her phone down. It ALERTS her with a text. She quickly picks it back up. Her eyebrows buckle.

CLOSE-UP: "We need to talk."

Chloe types.

CLOSE-UP: "When?"

INT. TANIA'S APARTMENT - MORNING

CLOSE-UP: Cell Screen. "When?"

Widen. Modern. Sleek. Lots of Latin touches. Family is important here.

                    TANIA
          Now.

                    SIRI
          I didn't quite get that.

                    TANIA
          NOW!

The cell sits in the palm of one hand. Tania's other hand has grown claws as long as Wolverine's. The nails have punctured her pillow. She stands in a ripped pajamas.

INT. DENTIST'S OFFICE - MORNING

Typical. Elevator music plays in the background. Francesca sits in a chair. A DENTIST, 50s, enters. He reads her file.

                    DENTIST
          Francesca, you were just in for a
          cleaning.

Francesca, mouth shut tightly, nods quickly. He sits.

                    DENTIST
          So what's bothering you?

Francesca remains tight-lipped. She points to her mouth.

                    DENTIST
          Let's have a look. Open wide...

She opens her mouth...

EXT. DENTIST'S OFFICE - MOMENTS LATER

A blinding white light ERUPTS from a window.

                    DENTIST (O.S.)
          Aaaaah!

INT/EXT. VAN SWOON TOWERS - SAME TIME

The black tower looms over the city.

                    OLGA (O.S.)
          I founded this company!

INT. OLGA'S OFFICE - CONTINUOUS

This room is a shrine to Olga. She stands in front of a wall-sized aquarium of piranhas.

The same group of shareholders make a wall in front of her.

> STEWART
> Your buyout will be quite generous.

> BOARDMEMBER
> Especially in light of recent
> events.

Lays open files on each of the models.

> STEWART
> You tampered with their lives.

> OLGA
> The models will be fine. And if
> they aren't, they're replaceable! I
> on the other hand, am not!

The shareholders put on their hats and leave.

The piranhas have gathered together in one area of the tank in back of Olga. She SLAMS her fist against the glass. They scatter.

EXT. CAFE - DAY

Posh. A place where only "the in-crowd" eats.

Chloe, Tania, and Francesca, in disguise, sit at a table. A WAITER pours water. He makes eyes at them.

> CHLOE
> Okay we've waited long enough for
> Max.

> TANIA
> I texted her twice.

> MAX (O.S.)
> I got them, Tania.

The girls jump back. After a few GRUNTS, MAX MATERIALIZES in the fourth chair. The other three are stunned.

> CHLOE
> We need to talk somewhere... more
> private.

                    MAX
          Why? I just got here.

                    FRANCESCA
          You're naked. And you have dimples
          in the wrong places.

Max looks down. *Yep, she's naked.* And it hits her like a ton
of bricks. The girls quickly leave. They try to cover Max's
body with menus.

INT. HOTEL - FRANCESCA'S SUITE - LATER

The girls sit. Francesca bags all of the empty water bottles.
Not thinking Tania bites a nail, hurts her mouth. Francesca
starts to laugh but suppresses it.

                    MAX
          It must be the cosmetics.

The girls look at her.

                    CHLOE
          How do you know?

                    MAX
          Hair color. Nail Polish. Lip Gloss.
          Concealer. We were fine before Dr.
          Fantanburger used the
          Transapplicatior. I need to find
          out what it really does.

                    CHLOE
          I need to talk to Ms. Van Swoon.

                    TANIA
          We're all in this together, Chloe.

Chloe looks at the other three. Max fades in and out.

                    CHLOE
          Just this once. And thanks, now I
          have that stupid song from *High
          School Musical* in my head.

INT. HOTEL - LOBBY - MOMENTS LATER

Like the Ritz. Elevator doors open. Three walk out followed
by Max, who is invisible, and wears a denim jumpsuit. Chloe
hums "We're All in This Together" from *High School Musical*.

                    MAX (INVISIBLE)
          Stop!

The three stop. Hordes of Reporters, including Noelle in
front, wait outside.

                    CHLOE
          What do we do?

                    MAX
          Disappear.

                    FRANCESCA
          Easy for you to say.

EXT. HOTEL - ALLEY - MOMENTS LATER

Door opens. The four rush out.

                    FRANCESCA
          I get us cab.

                    CHLOE
          Francesca, no!

She ignores and runs off. Francesca stands in the middle of
the busy street waiting for a cab. She waves. And yells:

                    FRANCESCA
          TAXI!

CRASH! WHAM! The bright light that ERUPTS from her mouth
causes a taxi pile up. Chloe turns to the other two.

                    CHLOE
          We'll walk.

The four turn up the street.

EXT. ANOTHER ALLEY - SAME TIME

ENRIQUE runs for his life. He looks for an exit. Tries to
climb a wall. Trips over garbage cans. He turns.

                    ENRIQUE
          Stay away from me!

A HOODED FIGURE stumbles toward him. He pulls out his wallet.

                    ENRIQUE
          Take it all.

                         TESA
                      (desperate)
              I don't want your money. I need--

She pulls down her hood.

TESA'S POV: Enrique ducks. Before he can get behind the
garbage can, a laser beam rockets from Tesa...

                         TESA
              -- Your help.

She slumps.

EXT. STREET - DAY

Sam waits at a hotdog stand. A chubby VENDOR fixes a dog.

                         SAM
              Everything.

The Vendor piles it on. POLICE CARS whiz by. Sam doesn't
notice, he's focused on the hotdog.

                         SAM
              I'll show Dad. More onions.

The Vendor looks at the dog, which is smothered. More
Policemen run past. Sam pays the Vendor. He turns. His mouth
drops open... his hotdog slips out.

SAM'S POV: Police surround the alley.

He runs to it.

A POLICEWOMAN, 20s, stops him.

                         POLICEWOMAN
              Authorized personnel only.

Sam's taken aback.

                         SAM
              CSI: Angel City.

He quickly flashes his gym card. She looks at him, lets him
through.

Sam fumbles with his camera. He squeezes his way through the
crowd of cops.

Stops. His eyes widen. He snaps off a photo. Enrique has been
turned completely to stone.

INT. VAN SWOON TOWERS - OLGA'S OFFICE - NIGHT

Olga, holding a champagne, stares out over the city, planning... scheming.

BAM!

A large double door flies open. A MALE ASSISTANT runs in.

                    ASSISTANT
          I told them you didn't
          want to be disturbed.

                    OLGA
     Who?

A section of Chloe's hair grabs the Assistant and tosses him aside.

Francesca, Tania and Max (we can only see her head and clothes) enter...

                    TANIA
          That would be us.

Tania tries to free her nails from the punctured door. Olga walks toward the girls.

                    OLGA
              (to: Assistant)
          That'll be all, Daniel.

The Secretary leaves. The girls approach her.

                    CHLOE
          What did *Superheroine* and that
          Transgender--

                    MAX
          Transapplicator.

                    CHLOE
          That... do to me?

Francesca threatens Chloe with her mouth.

                    CHLOE
     Us.

Olga leers... her gears are turning.

                    OLGA
          Apparently something gloriously
          unexpected.

38.

She finishes her champagne...

INT. TESA'S APARTMENT - NIGHT

Tesa climbs in through a window. The hood still hides her.
Sobbing, she drops onto the couch.

Something moves in her hood. Tesa KICKS over a table... sends
it flying into a mirror. *CRACK!*

                    TESA
          Francesca was right. I'm a beast...

She stares at the shattered mirror, eyes glowing. She pulls
down the hood.

Tesa has been transformed into a green creature with scales
and snake eyes. Live snakes slither about on her head.

                    TESA
          I look like Medusa.

The snakes spring into action. They whisper in her ear. Tesa
turns toward one, caresses another.

                    TESA
          What?

More snakes move about her head. Whispering.

                    TESA
          Come on? I'm pretty?

Her tears become sniffles. The snakes WHISPER in both of her
ears.

                    TESA (MEDUSA)
          Yes, yes you may be right.
              (more confident)
          You think I could be a cover girl?
          Like Chloe?
              (even more confident;
               sinister)
          No. Better than Chloe.

A snake comes within inches of her ear. Its forked tongue
darting in and out of her canal.

                    MEDUSA
          I do believe we are in need of a
          spa day.

She caresses more of the snakes, her voice becomes more
commanding...

INT. HERALD - MR. BLAKE'S OFFICE - DAY (LATE MORNING)

Mr. Blake addresses several reporters.

                    MR. BLAKE
          Five hair stylists and a cat turned
          to stone. And how many pictures?

The group remains silent. He holds up a lap top, The
Exhibitor. The front page has a shot of a stone victim. The
headline reads: Angel City rocks!

                    MR. BLAKE
          Angel City Rocks!?! C'mon people,
          what do I pay you for? I'm trying
          to sell news here before I really
          have to sell The Herald.

Sam bursts in waving his camera.

                    SAM
          Dad!

                    MR. BLAKE
          I told you not to call me that!

Sam hands him a photo. It's a picture of Enrique in the
alley. Mr. Blake beams. He puts an arm around Sam.

                    MR. BLAKE
          They beat us to it. Nice try.

Noelle turns to go out the door.

                    MR. BLAKE
          Noelle, where are you going?

                    NOELLE
          Still trying to get a lead on what
          happened to the four Van Swoon
          models. No one's seen them since
          the launch party.

                    MR. BLAKE
          Take Sam with you.

Sam's eyes pop open as he takes in Noelle's shapely body.

                    NOELLE
          But I have Jamal.

                         MR. BLAKE
          Not anymore.

Her glare meets Sam's eager face.

EXT. DESERT - DAY (AFTERNOON)

A Lear Jet, with a Van Swoon logo, lands on the runway. It
comes to a stop near the hanger. A jetway is rolled against
it. Doors open. Chloe, Max, Tania and Francesca, carrying
suitcases, walk down the stairs... followed by Olga.

A hummer drives up to meet them.

Max continues down the stairs. She fades in and out.

                         CHLOE
          Why couldn't we just get a shot?

                         MAX
          Because a shot doesn't cure
          whatever the Transapplicator did to
          us.

Chloe's hair sways wildly - one section shooting one way, one
expanding to the size of a Yoga ball.

                         CHLOE
          Stop already!?!

The hair freezes in position. Chloe notices.

                         CHLOE
          What I wouldn't do for a ponytail.

The hair leaps into motion, shrinking and tying itself into a
tight bun. Chloe looks on amazed and satisfied.

                         CHLOE
               Hmm!

Tania hands her suitcase to the Driver. He goes to take it,
but Tania doesn't let go. They both look down to see her
large nails have punctured the handle.

Olga rushes past them.

                         OLGA
          Snell, ladies, snell. We have
          absolutely no time to waste.

INT/EXT. HUMMER - CONTINUOUS

The girls look out the window as the hummer drives across the desert. As they come over a ridge, Chloe notices a sign which says, "PRIVATE FACILITY, NO TRESPASSING."

She turns to Olga, who sits across from the girls.

>   MAX
>   You own all of this?
>
>   OLGA
>   Oh my dear, this is just one of Van
>   Swoon's R&D sites. We have several
>   around the globe.

Olga smiles. The Hummer turns a corner.

MOMENTS LATER

The Hummer comes to a stop in front of the facility. The girls climb out.

>   OLGA
>   Welcome to your chateau away from
>   chateau. Entrez-vous.

TWO WHITE STEEL DOORS glide open. Dr. Fantanburger emerges. Turns to two TECHNICIANS who have joined them.

>   DR. FANTANBURGER
>   Prep them.

INT. SPA - DAY (AFTERNOON)

Busy. Beyond upscale. WOMEN in towels and robes hustle back and forth. Sam's eyes could POP out of his head.

>   SAM
>   Where do we start?
>
>   NOELLE
>   *You're* going to start by waiting
>   out here. I'm going to do a little
>   investigative reporting and a
>   seaweed wrap.
>
>   SAM
>   But--

                    NOELLE
          Sam look around, Van Swoon's models
          used to come here. If I'm going to
          get any leads, I'm going to have to
          blend in.

Sam watches a statuesque blonde walk by in just a towel.

                    SAM
          I can blend in.

Noelle gives him a look: *"Yeah, right."*

They approach the desk. An SNOTTY RECEPTIONIST looks Noelle
over.

                    NOELLE
          I'm here for the Lavender Marine
          Bolus Massage. The name is Hardy.
          Noelle Hardy, the famous Herald
          reporter.

                    SNOTTY RECEPTIONIST
          I get my news from Buzzfeed.

Sam snickers. The doors open behind them...

A hooded Medusa enters.

                    SECURITY GUARD
          Sorry, Miss. Closing time.

A green laser beam rockets from her eyes, turning the guard
to stone.

Noelle and Sam turn. They freeze. As do others.

                    MEDUSA
          Bonjour, mes amies! I understand
          this spa has group specials.

She pulls back her hood revealing her head of snakes.

Mayhem. Women run and SCREAM. Four BEEFY MASSEUSES rush her.
She fires her beams, turning them to stone.

                    MEDUSA
          Consider them my contribution to
          your sculpture garden. A Medusa
          original.

Medusa sends them flying into the columns with ease. She
turns a few more victims to stone.

Sam grabs Noelle by the wrist. They hide behind the
receptionist's desk.

                    NOELLE
          Shouldn't you be taking pictures?

                    SAM
          Right.

Sam stands up as more bodies fly past him. He aims the camera
at Medusa. She grabs a robe from the snotty receptionist.

                    MEDUSA
          I read one could discover their inner
          chi here. I *really* need to find mine.

The Snotty receptionist nods slowly.

Sam snaps off a couple of photos. This catches Medusa's
attention. A snake lowers from her head, becomes large and
slides Medusa to Sam.

Sam looks for a place to run. He turns... turns again...
comes face-to-face with Medusa. She smiles. He drops to his
knees, praying.

                    SAM
          Don't turn me to stone. Please
          don't turn me to stone.

Medusa brushes a nail under his chin.

                    MEDUSA
          I wouldn't dream of it, cutie. I
          thought you might want a close-up.

Sam looks down at Noelle, who motions for him to take it,
then back at Medusa.

                    MEDUSA
          I don't have all day...

She smiles. Sam takes the shot.

INT. LAB

The girls float in suspended states while rings of pulsating
light scan their bodies. THE GRIDDED COMPUTER HEAD floats
over each girl, assessing floating data.

44.

OBSERVATION ROOM - SAME TIME

Olga and Dr. Fantanburger study the monitors.

> DR. FANTANBURGER
> This is all my fault.

> OLGA
> Hugo, focus on the positive. Four
> beautiful creatures. Thought to be
> perfect. But now they've been
> elevated to an entirely new stage --
> a whole new level of perfection. A
> creation only a God could make.

Dr. Fantanburger watches the numbers and samples.

> DR. FANTANBURGER
> I'm no god.

> OLGA
> *(smiles)*
> I wasn't talking about you.

Dr. Fantanburger pushes a microphone button.

> DR. FANTANBURGER
> Computer, report preliminary
> diagnostics.

The Computer head disappears from downstairs. Appears
upstairs by Fantanburger and Olga. Floating three-dimensional
diagrams of the models appear in front of him and Olga.

> COMPUTER
> All four women have experienced a
> fundamental DNA alteration due to
> the nanobots' Alpha Rays exposure.

> DR. FANTANBURGER
> Is the process reversible?

The computer remains silent.

> COMPUTER
> Inconclusive.

Fantanburger's head lowers. Olga beams. She turns to leave.

> OLGA
> Run more tests. Money is no object.

> DR. FANTANBURGER
> What kind of tests?

Olga spins around and leers.

> OLGA
> You did say *Superheroine* stands up
> to the elements. Let's see if they
> live up to its name.

She leaves. Fantanburger looks down at the girls. Guilt washes over his face.

INT. VAN SWOON LABS - DINING ROOM - DAY (AFTERNOON)

A dozen or so TECHS eat. Others serve themselves at the buffet. Chloe, Max and Tania sit at the table. Chloe's hair spreads butter on her cracker. Tania eats a sushi roll off of each of her nails.

Francesca walks over carrying a tray full of salad.

> FRANCESCA
> Bonjourno.

The three duck under the table. No light emerges from Francesca's mouth. She taps her teeth.

> FRANCESCA
> Courtesy of Dottor Fantanburger.
> Keeps the *'Shimmer Simmer'* in.
> > *(she lifts the mouth guard
> > off)*
> See?

Bright light envelopes the table. The girls cover their eyes.

> FRANCESCA
> Scusa!

The girls climb back into their chairs. Max looks down at Tania's nails.

> MAX
> Tania... where are your nails?

Tania looks down at her hands. Her long nails are gone. All that remains is skin. Before Tania can answer, something RUMBLES above.

The girls look up simultaneously. Tania's nails hang from the ceiling. They lock eyes, then look up again. The section of ceiling shakes. The girls scramble.

BAM!

The ceiling collapses onto the table, crushing it. The other
employees turn to the girls.

                    CHLOE
          I think we need a PA.

                    MAX
          They don't have PA's in labs.

Tania looks down at her nails. They've regenerated - normal
and red. She looks at them, then the hole above.

INT. VAN SWOON LABS - LAB - NIGHT

Empty. Doors slide open. Dr. Fantanburger enters.

                    COMPUTER
          Working late, Dr. Fantanburger?

He lays his files down on a console. Rolls a chair over. He
rubs his eyes.

                    COMPUTER
          The human active state begins
          deterioration rapidly on less than
          eight to ten hours of sleep.

Dr. Fantanburger opens a file... yawns.

                    DR. FANTANBURGER
               (terse)
          Thank you. Run today's results.

Floating blood pressure and heart beat numbers materialize
and float in the air around Fantanburger.

                    COMPUTER
          Your dilated pupils indicate your
          stress is high. Perhaps sleep--

                    DR. FANTANBURGER
          -- Just--

Silence. Four colorful strands of DNA appear around
Fantanburger casting a light on his face.

                    DR. FANTANBURGER
          It's becoming permanent.

He notices something flashing on his screen. It simply is a
file which says, "SUPERHEROINE." He clicks on it.

A RED "LOCKED" FLASHES around him.

                    DR. FANTANBURGER
          Computer, open this file.

                    COMPUTER
          That file is classified.

Fantanburger frowns.

                    DR. FANTANBURGER
               Override.

The word "CLASSIFIED" blinks menacingly.

INT. HERALD - MR. BLAKE'S OFFICE - DAY (MORNING)

Sam and Noelle sit in front of a beaming Mr. Blake. Mr. Blake
leaps up, looks at a poster size pic of Medusa.

                    MR. BLAKE
          Medusa. I love it. Goddess from
          hell. Snake charmer. She's green.
          Is she for the environment? I want
          to know. And if I want to know our
          readers want to know.
               (hugs them tightly)
          I want these headlines covering the
          city! My god, I'm a genius.

TIGHT: Computer Screen. Herald Front Page. SNAKE EYES!

INT. TESA'S APARTMENT - SAME TIME

Medusa sits on her couch. She reads the same article on the
laptop. She yelps and a snake punches the screen.

EXT. VAN SWOON LABS - TRACK - DAY (MORNING)

The girls jog in place and stretch at a starting line. Dr.
Fantanburger, surrounded by TECHNICIANS, studies monitors.

                    DR. FANTANBURGER
          This is a test of endurance.

                    FRANCESCA
          Essere pazzo! Running makes
          Francesca testy. You no like me
          testy.

                    MAX
          Dr. Fantanburger?

                    DR. FANTANBURGER
          Yes, Max?

                    MAX
          When can we see the empirical data--

Chloe mouths empirical to Tania. She shrugs.

                    MAX
          -- from the tests? We've been at
          this for several days now.

Fantanburger shifts.

                    DR. FANTANBURGER
          Soon. Now if you would...

He motions for them to line up. Max keeps her eyes trained on
Fantanburger.

EXT. VAN SWOON LABS - WEAPONS AREA - SAME TIME

A sign says, "RESTRICTED." In a bunker, SCIENTISTS hustle
back and forth. Five klicks away is a missile on a launchpad.

A TECH, wearing a headset, counts down.

                    TECH
          Three, two, one...

More Technicians push buttons, flip switches etc.

-- THE MISSILE ROARS TO LIFE AND TAKES OFF.

EXT. VAN SWOON LABS - TRACK - SAME TIME

Dr. Fantanburger FIRES a starter pistol. The girls run.

THE MISSILE barrels into the sky. The scientists CLAP... a
successful mission.

THE GIRLS run on the track, each trying to outdo the other.
Francesca elbows Chloe. A section of Chloe's hair trips
Francesca. Francesca singes it. Max and Tania shake their
heads.

In the bunker, an alarm BLARES. Followed by another. A
Technician looks up from his monitor

                    TECHNICIAN
          It's off course!

The scientists run to the radar.

                    SCIENTIST
          Evacuate the facility!

ALARMS CLANG. Dr. Fantanburger looks up from his monitors.

The girls continue to race. Tania and Max slow down.
Francesca and Chloe continue to vie for number one.

More hair EXTENDS from Chloe, blocking Francesca's view.
Chloe smells something. She turns, realizes Francesca is
burning a hole through her hair.

                    CHLOE
          Ow! Italian Slunt!

Francesca can finally see... her eyes open wide.

                    FRANCESCA
          Oh Merda!

                    CHLOE
          Don't you call me a, "merda!"
          What's a merda anyway?

Francesca points.

                    CHLOE
          Oh.

Francesca turns in the other direction, runs. Chloe looks.
The missile heads directly toward the field. She bolts. The
missile closes in on the four girls.

                    MAX
          We're never going to make it!

Tania looks around. Francesca trips. Chloe goes to pick her
up. The shadow of the missile covers them. They crouch.

                    CHLOE
          Francesca, I'm sorry for every mean
          thing I ever said about you.

                    FRANCESCA
          Francesca accepts.

                    CHLOE
          Aren't you sorry about anything you
          said about me?

                    FRANCESCA
          No. You are bloated. And old.

The missile's nose heads directly for them. Tania turns
around. She closes her eyes.

Chloe looks up. The missile closes and stops.

Silence.

Chloe opens her eyes. Her hair has expanded to the size of a
large circus net. The missile balances on her hair.

Dr. Fantanburger peeks from behind one of his monitors.

                    DR. FANTANBURGER
          Ipso Lorem.

Tania and Francesca look on in awe. Max reappears,
disbelieving.

-- Its engines FIRE up, pushing Chloe into the ground.

                    CHLOE
          Get it off! Get it off of me!

Tania and Francesca spring into action. Max joins Chloe.

                    MAX
          Throw it!

                    CHLOE
          How?!

                    MAX
          Think!

-- Chloe's HAIR MORPHS INTO A HAIR HAND. It throws the
missile up into the air.

-- Tania aims her hands at it. And FIRES her "naillets."

The nails fly through the air, puncturing the engine. Tania
turns to Francesca.

                    TANIA
          Now!

-- Francesca opens her mouth. It glows brighter and brighter.
It turns white hot. A huge burst of white light EXPLODES.

-- Dr. Fantanburger'S monitor for Francesca registers: 15,000
degrees.

Her Shimmer Simmer Blast reaches the missile. BOOM!

It explodes.

The girls dive. They're stunned. Chloe slowly gets up. She
turns to Tania. They laugh nervously. Francesca comes over.
She inserts her mouth guard and joins the nervous laugh.

> MAX
> Hey guys!

They turn to her.

> MAX
> We did it--

-- A missile wing falls out of the sky and CRUSHES Max.

KA-BLAMMMMMMMM!

They're horrified.

Max reappears. The chunk went through her. She looks down and
faints. Chloe turns to Tania and Francesca.

> CHLOE
> Oh Emm Gee, we're not models--

> TANIA
> -- We're supermodels!

> CHLOE
> Line stealing slunt.

INT. VAN SWOON TOWER - SAME TIME

Olga, drink in hand, observes the girls on a large monitor.
She gleams. She taps a blue tooth in her ear.

> OLGA
> Tell our global partners that the
> price just went up.

INT. FASHION MAGAZINE HEADQUARTERS - DAY (AFTERNOON)

Beyond hip. Way beyond. A SECRETARY juggles a Starbucks
coffee tray with files as she tries to open the door. She
finally manages to open it.

Her tray drops. Files spill on top of spreading coffee.

The entire magazine staff has been turned to stone.

In another elevator, a livid Medusa stews. The doors close.

52.

INT. VAN SWOON LABS - HALL - LATER

The girls triumphantly parade past various labs and rooms.

>   CHLOE
>   Did you see the way I threw that
>   missile? Um-azing!

>   TANIA
>   What's "um-azing" is how you
>   conveniently forget those were my
>   nails cutting the engine loose and
>   Shimmer's smile over there making
>   it go boom.

>   FRANCESCA
>   Zee Shimmer. Mi piace.

The girls look at Francesca. She realizes she's smiling.
Returns to her 'tude look.

>   TANIA
>   And Max, the way you took that
>   wing... that was bad-ass. Max?

The girls look around. She's missing.

>   TANIA
>   Where's Max?

>   CHLOE
>   You sure she's not here?

Tania stops; waves her arms in back and front of her.
Missing.

INT. VAN SWOON LABS - TEST ROOM - SAME TIME

Fantanburger, joined by the floating computer head, talks to
Olga on a large monitor.

A door opens, unnoticed by all in the room. Max, invisible,
slinks closer to the conversation.

>   OLGA
>   Hugo, those girls are property of
>   Van Swoon Cosmetics. Soon to be the
>   property of our buyers. Who are on
>   their way.

>   DR. FANTANBURGER
>   They're human beings. Not property.

The monitor goes black. Fantanburger looks at the computer head. The door once again, quietly opens.

INT. VAN SWOON LABS - HALL - CONTINUOUS

Max materializes. Runs down the hallway. Realizes she's naked and runs into the ladies room...

INT. VAN SWOON LABS - MODELS' DORM - MOMENTS LATER

Sterile. Medical. Very non-model-like living. Francesca and Tania change. Chloe stares at herself in the mirror, changing hair colors -- red, black, blue, green... finally settling on blonde. Satisfied...

> CHLOE
> The world is back in balance.

The door opens. Max, invisible and wrapped in toilet paper like a mummy, rushes in. She materializes.

> MAX
> We have to go.

Francesca closes her closet door. Now in jeans and t-shirt, plops down on the bunk bed next to Tania.

> CHLOE
> We're in the desert. And not
> Coachella kind of desert either.

Max searches for a reason. *Ah Ha!* She points to the flatscreen TV hanging on the wall.

> MAX
> Sample sale!

The girls turn to the TV. A NEWSCASTER reports about a huge once-a-year designer sample sale. Chloe cocks her head.

> MAX
> Manolos. Half priced. Hello?

They stand upright.

INT. VAN SWOON LABS - CORRIDOR - LATER

The girls sneak around a corner. TWO GUARDS block their way. Francesca pops her mouth guard out. Chloe stops her.

                    CHLOE
          Don't hurt them.

She frowns, then aims her mouth at the security camera. And
fires a white PUFF. The camera melts.

IN A SECURITY ROOM, A GUARD watches a security console with
multiple screens. The screen where the girls are, goes white.
He picks up a phone. Something invisible CLOCKS him with it.

BACK IN THE CORRIDOR, Chloe gives Francesca the thumbs up.
Chloe peeks around the corner. Her hair ROCKETS out like two
hair arms. The hair wraps around both guards and pulls them
to the ground. She turns to Tania.

                    CHLOE
          Go... Hard Nails.

                    TANIA
          You're not the boss of me.

Tania leaps from behind the wall... crouches and aims a hand
at the door. Her index finger nail stretches the length of
the corridor into the lock... and picks it.

The girls run to the door. And open. They're free!

EXT. PARKING AREA - CONTINUOUS

The area is filled with Van Swoon Hummers. Max joins them.

                    MAX
          Time to add a little Concealer.

Max turns invisible, but her clothes remain visible.

                    CHLOE
          Ahem.

Max stops... realizes.

She strips and springs into action. Runs across the lot,
passes a sleeping SECURITY GUARD, and takes Hummer keys from
a wall of keys.

She wings them across the lot. Chloe catches them with a
small hair hand. The girls run to the Hummer.

INT. VAN SWOON LABS - LAB - SAME TIME

Fantanburger studies floating numbers and equations. He notices a computer monitor... which is focused on the outside perimeter.

He sees the girls piling into the Hummer. He goes to push a floating "lockdown" button.

He watches Tania toss Max her clothes. Chloe starts the engine.

He pulls his finger away from the button. The Hummer roars out of the parking lot.

INT. VAN SWOON LABS - HALL - LATER

Olga, flanked by a team of bodyguards who resemble a SWAT TEAM and her assistant, march to the girls' quarters. Dr. Fantanburger tries to keep up.

Olga manages a tight smile. Opens the door.

> OLGA
> Ladies, I have fantabulous news!

Her eyes sweep the empty room. Hands clench, forming fists.

> OLGA
> Find them.

INT/EXT. WAREHOUSE - DAY (AFTERNOON)

Crowded. This is the sample sale of the year. Juicy. Betsey Johnson. Versace. Ghost. Manolo. Ferragamo, Marc Jacobs, Fendi. You name it, it's here.

The girls stand in front, assessing the animalistic behavior of female sample sale shoppers.

> CHLOE
> Be fearless.

Francesca and Tania nod. Max looks worried. Tania lays a hand on her shoulder.

> TANIA
> Don't worry, girl. There's enough
> Maggy London to go around.

The girls rush into the sea of women tearing at clothes, hand bags and shoes. This is the ultimate girl fight.

Sam and Noelle enter.

                    NOELLE
          Sample sales. I hate sample sales.

                    SAM
          If your missing models are going to
          turn up, it'll be here. This place
          is as shallow as a three-foot pool.

TWO WOMEN, 20s, in their underwear fight over a dress in
front of them. Sam snaps off a pic with his camera.

                    SAM
          And shallow is good.

Francesca spies a pair of Jimmy Choo pumps on a rack. She
rushes for them. AN ASIAN WOMAN, 20s, also sees them. Just as
she is about to pick them up. She grabs her hand as it turns
red and SMOKES. She drops them.

                    ASIAN WOMAN
          Help! I'm on fire!

A SALES CLERK rushes to her aid. A victorious Francesca grabs
her shoes and tries them on.

Chloe turns a corner. Spots a Vivienne Westwood dress on a
rack. A RICH PARK AVENUE TYPE, 40s, is just about to pick it
up when WIND blows her hair.

Chloe's hair SNAPS back to her... dress in tow.

Tania and Max try on sunglasses. Tania notices Max's mood.

                    TANIA
          You gonna tell me what's up?

Before Max can answer...

BLAM! BLAM! BLAM!

In various areas of the warehouse - Chloe, Francesca, Noelle
and Sam, and Tania and Max turn.

A fashionable gang, holding automatic weapons, stand in the
center of the store. The leader, MARCELLAS, somewhat gay and
dressed outrageously, swings his stuff forward.

                    MARCELLAS
          Ladies, this is a very chic
          robbery. Now if you would be so
          kind as to give us all your money!

A WOMAN SCREAMS. Followed by another. And another. Marcellas
FIRES his gun in the air.

>   MARCELLAS
>   Screaming's so boorish. And
>   useless.

Max looks at Tania. Thinks fast. Tosses Tania sunglasses.
She disappears. Clothes strip quickly off.

>   TANIA
>   What are you--

Tania gets the idea. She puts on the glasses... takes two
more.

The Fashionasties continue to collect money. Chloe spies
Francesca, who's steaming - one of the gang's women just took
her pumps.

>   MARCELLAS
>   Well, well, well I should'a known
>   we were gonna get celebrity cash
>   today.

Chloe turns... stares into the gang's leader's eyes.

>   MARCELLAS
>   Chloe Connor! I am a fan--

CRACK!

Marcellas goes down from the punch. Chloe whips around. Max
partially materializes, waving her hand from the punch.

>   MAX
>   Ow!

>   TANIA
>   Put these on!

Tania joins them, hands Chloe the sunglasses.

>   CHLOE
>   I hate Donna Ricco.

>   MAX
>   Put them on!

Chloe thinks. Gets the idea.

>   CHLOE
>   Ohhhhhhhh...

58.

She puts them on. The three make eye contact with Francesca.
By their expressions, we know what's about to go down.

Marcellas, still rubbing his chin, runs to the front and
joins his gang.

                         MARCELLAS
               Who hit me?!

                         CHLOE (O.S.)
               Hey, Fan Boy!

The entire store turns. Chloe, Tania, Francesca block the
exit.

                         CHLOE
               I suggest you give that
               money back now, Mister.

Francesca glares at the girl with *her* shoes.

                         FRANCESCA
               No one takes Francesca's shoes.

The gang picks up their weapons. Clicks the releases. And
aims. Chloe looks over at Tania and Francesca. Tania turns to
Chloe.

                         TANIA
               How are we supposed to fight them?

Chloe thinks.

                         CHLOE
               Work it?

The girls spring into action amid a spray of bullets. Tania
leaps onto a cash register... FIRES her "naillets."

Francesca pops her mouth guard out and opens her mouth
pulsing white light - very targeted - rushes out. Their
bullets melt in mid-air.

Marcellas runs out of the warehouse to the getaway van.

He throws the door open.

WHOOSH! SLAM!

Something *YANKS* him to the ground. He turns around as Chloe's
hair returns to her... with the bags of money.

Chloe turns around.

The crowd looks at them stunned. Noelle elbows Sam.

> NOELLE
> Picture!

Max MATERIALIZES. Chloe hangs a dress in front of her to block her nudity.

> TANIA
> Selfie!

The girls take one on Tania's phone. They move.

> CHLOE
> Wait! What about one for safety?

The once frantic crowd breaks into WILD APPLAUSE. Sam makes his way through the throng and aims his camera.

The girls notice and SMILE!

FLASH!

INT/EXT. HUMMER - TRAVELING - LATER

Chloe weaves the Hummer in and out of traffic. Francesca, sitting shotgun, goes to check her lipstick. It's still red. She smiles. It's a girl party.

> CHLOE
> Did you see us?!

> TANIA
> Yeah, Streak, we were there...
> 'member?

Chloe looks down at her Vivienne Westwood dress in a bag.

> CHLOE
> I can't wait to try Vivienne on.

The girls nod in agreement. Max works up the nerve.

> MAX
> We can't go back.

SCREECH!

> CHLOE
> Why?

Chloe SLAMS on the brakes. The girls study Max.

60.

                    MAX
          I lied. I didn't really want to go
          shopping with you guys. Although I did
          find a nice Fendi bag. Van Swoon
          doesn't want to help us. She wants to
          sell us. And I'm guessing whoever it's
          to, it isn't an agency.

                    CHLOE
          Sell us as what?

                    MAX
          Weapons.

The mood turns glum.

                    CHLOE
          We should call the police.

                    MAX
          We're freaks. They'll lock us up
          first. Then dissect us.

                    FRANCESCA
          I burn anyone who cuts Francesca.

                    TANIA
          Max, what about your house?

                    MAX
          That's putting my mother at risk.

Chloe thinks. Then...

                    CHLOE
          I have a place. A safe house...

She starts the engine. Drives the Hummer.

                    TANIA
          This could have a tracking device.

Tania fires a flurry of nails at the dashboard. It smokes.

INT. MODELING AGENCY - DUSK

TIGHT: Computer Screen. The Herald Front Page: "Mysterious
"Supermodels" save Donna Karan." By Noelle Hardy. The photo
Sam took sits underneath.

Green scaly hands gently close the laptop.

Medusa storms out. All models and staff have been turned to stone.

INT/EXT. CHLOE'S FIRST APARTMENT - DUSK

A neighborhood that resembles Queens. Brick building. A consignment shop, with a second floor apartment, stands by El tracks.

                    TANIA (O.S.)
          Wow. Who'd of thought you...

Inside, it's just as modest. Ikea furniture. Crates. Futon. The girls, shocked, stand in the middle, while Chloe makes tea.

                    TANIA
          ... would live here?

Chloe turns the burner on. Francesca tries to sit on a bean bag chair with no luck. She rolls over.

                    CHLOE
          It was my first apartment when I
          left Madison.

                    MAX
          You're from Wisconsin?

                    CHLOE
          Yes and I like cheese and Cracker
          Barrel. I come back when I really
          need to get away.

Max turns on a modest TV.

                    MAX
          Basic cable? Talk about roughing
          it.

Chloe takes mugs out of a cabinet. Half-smiles. Max spies a framed photo of a younger Chloe posing with her dad and mom. Her dad is a cop.

                    MAX
          Your dad was a cop?

Chloe's hair rushes to Max, grabs the picture. It returns to her. She looks at it, missing her parents.

                    CHLOE
          Police Chief of Madison.

                    TANIA
          Maybe he could help us.

                    CHLOE
          He's dead. They both are.

The group remains silent. Chloe's hair returns it gently to
the shelf. The tea pot whistles.

                    CHLOE
          Tea's ready.

                    TANIA
          We need a plan.

Little blasts of white puff from Francesca's mouth.

                    FRANCESCA
          Francesca's career is over.

Chloe takes her dress out of the bag... studies it.

                    MAX
          And don't forget that photographer
          snapped a pic of us. Olga's
          probably already seen it.

Chloe smiles. Her hair STRETCHES to the TV. Turns it off.

                    MAX
          Hey!

She bounces giddily to the girls.

                    CHLOE
          I have a way to revive our careers.
          And put us on the cover of every
          magazine again!

The girls are silent.

                    CHLOE
          We'll become Supermodels.

                    FRANCESCA
          Francesca is a supermodel already.

                    CHLOE
          Not that kind of supermodel. I
          mean. Hard Nails. Concealer.
          Shimmer. And me - Streak.

                    TANIA
          I think that hair color seeped into
          your brain. What are we going to do
          as supermodels?

                    CHLOE
          Fight crime, silly! Get it? We're
          super and we're models!

Francesca bursts out laughing. Sends a WHITE BEAM across the
room, blackening the stove.

                    FRANCESCA
          'Scusa.

                    TANIA
          We're not crime fighters.

Max thinks.

                    MAX
          Maybe Chloe's right.

Chloe turns to Max... stunned.

                    CHLOE
          You do, slun - Max?

                    MAX
          What if we were given these powers
          for a reason? Maybe this is a
          chance to give women a good reason
          to look up to us instead of for our
          looks.

                    CHLOE
          I just want to get back on *Teen
          Vogue* again.

                    FRANCESCA
          You are far too old for *Teen Vogue*.

Francesca and Tania nod. Max shakes her head. Chloe beams.

                    CHLOE
          Supermodels! Work it!

DISCO MUSIC UP: Supermodels! Theme Song

> RUPAUL TYPE SINGER
> *Streak can do anything with her
> long, beautiful hair/Shimmer can
> blind you with her smile if you
> stare/Hard Nails can fire bullets
> with the wave of her hand/Concealer
> can turn invisible just because she
> can...*

MONTAGE:

A gang of Robbers throws an exit door open and bolt to a waiting helicopter. They stop as a sunglass wearing Francesca, dressed in uber-hot clothes, blocks their way. They aim and FIRE.

"Naillets" knock their guns out of their hands. Tania, also wearing sunglasses, leaps. White hair snatches the guns out of their hands... returns to Chloe. And finally Max (invisible) SLUGS the helicopter pilot.

> SINGERS
> *Fighting bad guys and their evil
> ways/ Together we'll prove crime
> doesn't pay/Supermodels! work
> it/Save the world and look good
> doing it/Supermodels! work it/Save
> the world and look good doing it...*

A car chase turns onto a bridge over a river. As the cops and bad guys SHOOT it out, Max's head appears in the passenger seat with the robbers. An arm appears and grabs the steering wheel. The back tires melt as Francesca emits her *Simmer Shimmer* blast.

A LITTLE GIRL cries and points to her cat stuck in a tree. Naillets cause the branch to CRACK and fall to the ground. The cat falls off, but Streak's hair catches it.

Sam snaps off more pics of The Supermodels! in action.

OLGA barks orders at her swat team to find the Supermodels!

Seeing these photos, drives Medusa into a frenzy in her lair. A snake tosses a lap top.

CHLOE'S HAIR WIPES TO BLACK.

INT. CHLOE'S FIRST APARTMENT - NIGHT

A TV plays. Tania, sitting on the couch, turns around.

                    TANIA
          We're on TV!

The other three pounce. Each jockey for the best seat on the
couch... elbows, grunts etc. Chloe's hair pushes the other
three to the sides of the couch.

                    CHLOE
          My couch.

                    FRANCESCA
          Shhhhh.

They turn to the TV. A MALE NEWSCASTER speaks to camera. Four
pretty silhouettes float behind him.

                    NEWSCASTER
          Today, more reports came in about
          the four mysterious superheroines
          who have been busting crime all
          over Angel City. Katie Ward has
          more.

ON TV: KATIE WARD, holds a microphone, talking to camera.

                    KATIE WARD
          Thanks, Bill. The entire Angel City
          Heights section is buzzing about
          the four attractive superheroes
          that have been nicknamed The
          Supermodels! Earlier tonight this
          building in back of me was an
          inferno. The Fire Department had
          all but given up until... Let's go
          to the video.

IN THE APARTMENT: the girls lean in. Chloe STOMPS her feet up
and down.

                    CHLOE
          There I am!

ON TV: The building is now an inferno. Firemen run out. The
broadcast has on-screen text that reads: "Earlier Tonight."

                    FIREMAN
          She's gonna blow! Get back!

The Supermodels! arrive on the scene. Francesca aims her
mouth at a nearby water tower. Chloe stops her and points.

                    CHLOE
          Eew! Angel City Tap.

They look around. Chloe smiles. She spots a VOSS WATER
delivery truck. Her hair reaches out and picks it up. She
tosses the truck into the air.

                    CHLOE
          Now!

Francesca aims her mouth and FIRES. The truck explodes.
Designer water cascades down onto the fire, putting it out.

The Supermodels! blow kisses and run off.

                    KATIE WARD
          And it's reports like these all
          over town that are turning these
          urban legends into real ones.

IN THE APARTMENT: the girls turn to each other.

                    MAX
          As Chloe would say, Oh Emm Gee.

                    TANIA
          This is so bomb.

Francesca nods. Chloe walks to the a stack of magazines. It's
just her on the cover. Max turns from the couch to Chloe.

                    MAX
          Chloe, we're becoming famous.

Chloe looks at a couple of her magazines.

                    CHLOE
          Um-mazing.

She grabs her bag.

                    TANIA
          Where are you going?

                    CHLOE
          Get some air.

                    FRANCESCA
          Do you desire Francesca's company?

                    CHLOE
          Not right now.

Chloe opens the door... sighs and leaves.

INT. VAN SWOON TOWERS - NIGHT

Olga looks at the neon skyline. The door opens. Olga's
Assistant leads a humble Fantanburger in.

> OLGA
> Leave us.

The Assistant closes the doors behind her.

> DR. FANTANBURGER
> You wanted to see me?

Olga sighs... walks to her bar by the piranha tank. Pours a
drink. Takes a sip. Points a remote at four monitors. The
Supermodels! appear paused in each one.

> OLGA
> You could've stopped them, Hugo.

She takes a sip. Fantanburger shifts.

> OLGA
> But you didn't. You cost me your
> trust. And you cost me my word.
> Which was highly regarded.

Fantanburger shifts.

> DR. FANTANBURGER
> They're just girls. Not weapons.

> OLGA
> But worse than that... you cost me
> money. Billions of dollars. Now
> trust can eventually be re-built.
> But lost money is an entirely
> different story.

Olga pushes a green button underneath her desk. Without
warning, the ceiling parts, a mechanical arm drops down,
clamps Fantanburger by the leg and carries him over to the
piranha tank, which slides out from the wall.

The fish swim to the surface, anticipating their dinner. The
crane dangles Fantanburger over the hungry fish.

> DR. FANTANBURGER
> Please, there must be another way!

Olga's intercom buzzes. She presses the button.

> ASSISTANT (O.S.)
> Ms. Van Swoon--

68.

                    OLGA
          -- I said I was not to be
          disturbed.

                    SECRETARY
          But--

                    OLGA
          -- Disturb me again and your first
          task tomorrow morning will be
          filing--

BOOM!

The doors fly open.

                    OLGA
          -- for unemployment.

Medusa stands in the doorway. Olga's finger moves slightly
away from the release button.

                    MEDUSA
          Consider yourself disturbed.

                    OLGA
          Tesa? I'm so glad you...
               (her fingers search around
               the panel for the
               security button)
          ... you're all right! I was
          concerned.

Medusa saunters toward Olga, whose finger moves to a red
button.

                    MEDUSA
          Don't bother with security dahling.
          They are how should I say? Stoned.

One of the snakes in her hair SPRINGS into action... leaps
over to Olga... blocking her finger. Olga's isn't phased. *Or
if she is, she's not going to show it.*

                    OLGA
          Hmm, interesting that you chose a
          God's name.

                    MEDUSA
          Nothing is random. As you will see
          when I become *America's Top Model.*

She points to her eyes... raises her eyebrows. Olga tries to
compose herself. Manages her tight smile.

                    OLGA
          America's Next Top Model?! What if
          I were to tell you I can show you
          an even greater purpose beyond
          such... surface desires?

Medusa moves deeper into the room.

                    OLGA
          I have a proposition for you...
          confrere.

Medusa glances at Fantanburger, who is dangling and shaking.
Her snakes extend and form a chair underneath her.

                    MEDUSA
          We're listening...

INT. BAR - NIGHT

Semi-crowded. Noelle and Sam sit at a table. Files and photos
spread out. Beers in front of them. As Noelle goes through
their info, Sam seems to be more interested in her.

                    NOELLE
          Okay here's what we've got. Four
          missing models.

She spreads the photos out of Chloe, Francesca, Tania and
Max.

                    NOELLE
          Now we have four supermodels.

She spreads their photos out. Sam's eyes dart from their
photos back to Noelle.

                    NOELLE
          Hey, "Picture Boy," are you paying
          attention?

                    SAM
          Yeah, yeah. Sure. I mean I wasn't
          for a hot sec. But now I am again.

He smiles. Noelle points to the photos.

                    NOELLE
          It has to be them. But how?

Sam brings out the photos from the *Superheroine* Launch. He
points to Fantanburger standing near Olga.

70.

                              SAM
                    Dr. Hugo Fantanburger?

She searches her notes. Stops.

                              NOELLE
                    Started off with NASA. Took a
                    supervisory role at The Genesis
                    Corporation. A Think Tank for the
                    Defense Department. Considered a
                    radical. Felt he could help
                    soldiers who lost limbs with
                    nanobot, Alpha Radiation
                    technology. Genesis is bought... by
                    Sun Dynamics. And who owns a major
                    chunk of Sun?

                              SAM
                    I know you're going to tell me.

Noelle leans in. Holds up Olga's photo.

                              NOELLE
                    What does a cosmetics maven need a
                    defense contractor for?

                              SAM
                    Fend off paparazzi?

Noelle smirks.

                              NOELLE
                    What?

                              SAM
                    You're kinda cute when you're
                    getting all Sherlock Holmesy.

Noelle stops. All business. Flustered.

                              NOELLE
                    There's also the matter of Medusa.
                    Who is she?

Noelle looks a pic of Olga and Tesa.

EXT. STREET - CONTINUOUS

Dark. Deserted. Sam looks around for a cab. Nothing. He
starts walking faster.

THREE SHADOWY FIGURES follow.

Sam whips around. Nothing. He walks faster. The wind kicks up.

CLICK! CLICK! CLICK!

The footsteps behind him pick up the pace as well. A bead of sweat rolls down Sam's distressed face. He turns a corner.

WHAM!

Sam runs into a HULKING SHADOWY FIGURE. The only white he sees is his leering smile and white eyes.

                    GOON ONE
          Where you going, Peter Parker?

                    SAM
          Uh-uh nowhere.

As Sam backs away the figure steps out of the shadows. This is a goon you don't want to meet at night or day. He wears a skull cap and his muscles bulge through his too-tight sweater.

                    GOON ONE
          He said he ain't going anywhere,
          boys. Good one.

The OTHER TWO GOONS, just as menacing, step out of the shadows into the street lamps.

                    GOON TWO
          Oh he's going somewhere.

                    GOON THREE
          Down.

Sam tries to find an exit.

                    SAM
          C'mon, guys. I'm just photographer.
          You guys probably make more on a
          single take than I do in a year.

They close in on him.

                    GOON ONE
          Our boss wants a word with you.

Sam crouches...

THWACK!

72.

A blur of WHITE HAIR wraps around Goon 3 and punches him into
the wall. The goons turn.

Chloe, sunglasses and hot mini-outfit, stands on a fire
escape.

                    CHLOE
          Hi.

                    GOON ONE
          Get her!

Chloe's hair springs into action. It rockets out grabbing
Goon One and slapping Goon Two.

                    CHLOE
          Oooh, hair's thinning, handsome.
          You might want to use a volumizer.

Goon Three rushes behind her, swinging a crowbar. Sam points.

                    SAM
          Look out!

Her hair forms a fist, and pops up...

BOOMP!

Goon Three goes down.

Chloe's hair grabs the other two goons and SLAMS them into
each other. Chloe stands over Goon One. He looks up at her,
dazed.

                    CHLOE
          Naughty.

Her Hair rockets down, PUNCHES him unconscious. She smiles.
Runs to Sam.

                    CHLOE
          Are you alright?

She helps Sam up. He nods slowly.

                    SAM
          I usually would have a smart ass
          come back, but I got nothing.

Chloe picks up his camera. Hands it to him.

                    CHLOE
          Here.

Sam takes it. She smiles.

                    CHLOE
          What?

                    SAM
          Are you Chloe Connor?

Chloe pauses.

                    CHLOE
          Isn't she blonde?

She flashes her winning grin. Sam aims his camera.

                    SAM
          Mind?

Chloe poses.

                    CHLOE
          How's this?

FLASH!

Sam checks his viewfinder. It's an awesome pic.

                    CHLOE
          Way better than Nigel.

                    SAM
          Who?

Silence. Sam looks up. She's gone.

INT. VAN SWOON TOWERS - BOARD ROOM - MORNING

A shareholder breakfast meeting is in progress The door
opens. Olga strolls in. Marshall turns toward her.

                    OLGA
          A breakfast meeting? The most
          important meal of the day.

She walks to the coffee. Pours herself a cup.

                    STEWART
          We fired you.

Olga takes a long sip. Circles the table like a predator.

                    OLGA
          Gentlemen... and ladies, I have
          decided to not accept the terms of
          your buy out. I feel I have far too
          much I still wish to accomplish
          with Van Swoon before I move on.

Stewart joins Marshall.

                    STEWART
          What are you trying to pull?

Olga smiles.

                    OLGA
          May I introduce you to my new VP?
          In charge of HR.

Medusa, hooded, enters. She pulls down her hood.

                    MEDUSA
          You're all fired. And it's written
          in stone.

She stretches out her arms. Her eyes glow. The snakes' eyes
glow. Beams bathe the room in green. The shareholders try to
run, but are instantly turned to stone.

Medusa admires her work.

                    MEDUSA
          I never grow tired of that.

                    OLGA
          Hmm.

Medusa pulls her hood back up.

                    MEDUSA
          My end of the bargain is complete.

                    OLGA
          Almost.

She taps a button on a control panel.

ON SCREEN: Sam's photo of Chloe. Medusa's snakes slither
about her head threateningly.

                    OLGA
          Bring them to me. We will crown
          your ascendency together... with
          their destruction.

Medusa smiles. She rises, turns and leaves. She stops in the
doorway. Turns back. Olga drinks her coffee.

INT. CHLOE'S FIRST APARTMENT - MORNING

The girls sit at breakfast as Chloe breaks one piece of toast
into quarters. Tania SLAMS her laptop down. Francesca sits at
the table pissed. Max talks on the phone.

                    TANIA
          Something you want to tell us?

Chloe, now blonde and in pigtails, drinks her coffee.

                    CHLOE
          Uh... no.

                    FRANCESCA
          We are team... no?

                    TANIA
          Not if you ask Streak here?

Max covers the cell's mouthpiece.

                    MAX
          Will you keep it down!?! Sorry,
          Mother. Not you.

INT. MAX'S HOUSE - KITCHEN - SAME TIME

Drusilla, robed, stands in the kitchen on the phone.

                    DRUSILLA
          When is this tour of yours over?

Max thinks.

                    MAX
          Might be sooner than I thought,
          Mother.

                    DRUSILLA
          I wish you were here. So many
          bizarre things are happening in
          Angel City. First, this Medusa.
          Who does her hair? Now these
          Supermodels. Who I might I add are
          getting way more coverage than you.
          You could take a hint. I wonder if
          they have an Instagram account.

Max rolls her eyes.

                    MAX
          I know.

There's a KNOCK at Drusilla's kitchen door.

                    DRUSILLA
          Have to go. Someone's at the door.
          Probably the Meter Man. He crushes
          on me so hard.

                    MAX
          Really?

                    DRUSILLA
          Come home soon. And take care of
          that pimple.

They hang up. Drusilla walks to the door.

KNOCK! KNOCK!

                    DRUSILLA
          Stop that boorish knocking.

BOOM!

The door SPLINTERS and BLOWS in. The force knocks Drusilla
onto the floor. Drusilla SCREAMS.

Medusa saunters in... pulls down her hood.

INT. CHLOE'S FIRST APARTMENT - SAME TIME

Chloe sits at her kitchen table. Busted.

                    TANIA
          I finally thought you were getting
          past your whole me, me, me.

Max looks at the paper. Francesca glances at her watch.

                    MAX
          Is that what you want, Chloe - to
          be on your own again?

                    CHLOE
          No. Yes. I don't know. This is all
          so new to me. You know once upon a
          time it was just me at Van Swoon.
          Then you came Tania. Then Max.
                    (MORE)

                    CHLOE (CONT'D)
          And Francesca. Suddenly, I went
          from hot to not.

                    MAX
          Is that what you think? We pull you
          down?

The girls shake their heads. Francesca rises. Tania turns.

                    TANIA
          Where are you going?

Francesca MUMBLES something.

                    MAX
          I didn't get that.

Francesca musters up the courage...

                    FRANCESCA
          I have a Red Carpet.

                    TANIA
          What?!

                    MAX
          Oh for the love of god!

Chloe smiles... points.

                    CHLOE
          See I'm not the only one!

Max invades Francesca's personal space.

                    MAX
          Where is your appearance?

                    FRANCESCA
          The new Angel City Mall.

Tania pulls up alongside Max.

                    TANIA
          How did you book a job?

                    FRANCESCA
          Mi-mi-agent?

                    TANIA
          As Shimmer or Francesca?

                    FRANCESCA
                  (mumbles)
          Shimmer?

                    MAX
          I can't believe you! You two are
          going to make it simple for Olga to
          find us.

                    FRANCESCA
          But he's mi agent!

                    TANIA
          By letting him know your identity
          you compromise all of us.
          Either all of us appear or none of
          us.

Francesca, upset, goes to pull her mouth piece out. Max grabs
her hand.

                    MAX
          If you do it, you're going to need
          braces.

Chloe snickers. Max's face invades her personal space.

                    TANIA
          Don't even think it.

Her smile quickly disappears...

INT. HERALD - MR. BLAKE'S OFFICE - DAY (MORNING)

Noelle and Sam stand over Mr. Blake. Noelle lays down the
photos.

                    NOELLE
          I know it's them.

She lays out the photo of Streak and Chloe.

                    NOELLE
          And Olga Van Swoon's behind it.

Mr. Blake studies the photos and Noelle's story.

                    MR. BLAKE
          We can't run this story yet.

                    NOELLE
          Why?

> MR. BLAKE
> You don't have proof. And no proof
> equals fake news. We have a
> reputation.

> NOELLE
> Look at the photos.

> MR. BLAKE
> Have you even talked to Van Swoon?

Noelle bites her lower lip. She points to Chloe and Streak.

> NOELLE
> This is Chloe Connor.

> MR. BLAKE
> What do you think, Sam?

Sam pauses. Looks from Noelle to his dad.

> SAM
> Chloe Connor is a blonde. This
> Streak has white hair. And wears
> sunglasses.

> NOELLE
> Sunglasses?!

> SAM
> Very nice sunglasses?

Noelle's glares at Sam.

INT. PRISON - MARCELLAS'S CELL - AFTERNOON

Unlike other cells, Marcellas has used what was available to
make his extremely fashionable. He lies on a lower bunk,
underneath a HULKING PRISONER doing a crossword puzzle,
reading a GQ from the '80s.

> MARCELLAS
> You know, I can rock the Member's
> Only Jacket.

> HULKING PRISONER
> Uh-huh.

Growing chaos can be heard O.S. Marcellas closes his
magazine, pays attention.

> MARCELLAS
> Riot?

> HULKING PRISONER
> Might be serving chili for lunch
> again.

Armed guards run by their cell. Followed by more. And more.

A green blast bathes the hallway. Marcellas and the prisoner continue to do their thing. Still oblivious, the same guards fly backwards, now turned to stone.

> HULKING PRISONER
> What's a four-letter word for love?

BLAM!

The cell doors are ripped off. Marcellas and the prisoner fall out of their bunks. Medusa, looking richer and more menacing than ever, stands in their doorway. Snakes slither this way and that way on her head.

> MEDUSA
> I am in need of your services.

Marcellas climbs out of his bunk.

> MARCELLAS
> I don't know but I know a six-
> letter word.

He starts to run off with Medusa. Stops and looks back at his cell-mate, who's pouting on his bunk.

> MARCELLAS
> Want to join?

The hulking prisoner jumps to the floor.

INT. NEW ANGEL CITY MALL - DAY (AFTERNOON)

A mall of modern marvel. Like nothing we've ever seen before. Like mixing the best of Vegas with the Beverly Center. Blinking lights. Expensive stores. Glass elevators.

Noelle and Sam rush through the mall.

> SAM
> You can speak to me now. It's been
> two hours. I'll treat you to an
> Auntie Annie's pretzel.

Noelle stops and turns.

                    NOELLE
          I'm your partner. We're supposed to
          have each other's backs. How could
          you do that to me?

Sam looks everywhere but at her.

                    SAM
          Cinnamon?

Noelle's eyes pierce through Sam.

                    SAM
          What if they don't want to be
          exposed?

                    NOELLE
          Don't want to be exposed!?! They're
          making freaking mall appearances!

She points to a crowd of Teen Girls and Fan Boys who have
gathered around an elaborate catwalk.

A FAMOUS TV HOST addresses them.

                    TV HOST
          We've all heard about their great
          deeds...

The Supermodels! wait behind a curtain. Chloe, steaming,
turns to the others.

                    CHLOE
          When this is over we are f-i-n-n--

                    MAX/CONCEALER
          Get a dictionary! And yes we are.

                    TANIA/HARD NAILS
          For real.

                    FRANCESCA/SHIMMER
          I call Mafia.

Ryan gets the excited crowd salivating even more.

                    TV HOST
          They're hot. They're strong. But
          did I say, "they're hot?" Here they
          are Angel City. Your Supermodels!

House MUSIC up. The curtains part. The girls jockey for
position again.

                    TV HOST
          Streak!

Chloe turns to the others. Her expression says, "See? Ha ha."
She marches out onto the catwalk.

                    TV HOST
          Shimmer!

Francesca struts out. The crowd goes wild.

                    TV HOST
          Concealer.

Max, hand on hip, swings her stuff out.

                    TV HOST
          And Hard Nails!

Tania bounces out, waving her hands.

The crowd goes wild for the Supermodels! They stop at the
edge of the stage. Pose. Wave. Blow kisses. The TV Host walks
in front of them. He turns to the crowd.

                    TV HOST
          Wow! I'm sweating up here! Okay
          we're going to take a few questions
          for them.

He points to a TEEN GIRL who holds a poster of them.

                    TEEN GIRL
          Streak, do you flat iron your hair
          before you fight crime or is it
          naturally straight?

                    CHLOE
          It's whatever I want it to be!
          Which goes to show all of you
          ladies can do anything you want!

She giggles. Sam snaps off a picture.

                    SAM
          She's so hot.

Noelle gives him the look. She raises her hand to ask a
question.

                    MEDUSA (O.S.)
          I have a question.

The group turns and GASPS. Noelle and Sam turn.

Medusa stands in the back with her arms folded. Her snakes
have extended and wrapped themselves around a glass elevator
full of frightened shoppers. The snakes on the other side of
her head dangle Drusilla from the top of the atrium.

                    MEDUSA
          Who do you save first? A group of
          strangers in an elevator?

The snakes RIP the elevator off its track. Shoppers SCREAM.

                    MEDUSA
          Or one of your own mothers?

Max looks up, recognizes...

                    MAX
          Mom?

Drusilla looks down. Recognizes...

                    DRUSILLA
          Maxine?! Help me!

Noelle catches this. Throws a sharp glance to Sam.

                    MEDUSA
          Also, does your hair thicken on its
          own?

This angers Francesca. She stomps her boot.

                    FRANCESCA
          Why does she get all the
          questions?! This is Francesca's
          appearance!

Chloe lowers her sunglasses slightly.

                    CHLOE
          Tesa?

                    MEDUSA
          There is no Tesa. Only Medusa!

Her snakes pitch the elevator of people to the stage and drop
Drusilla. The crowd panics. The models spring into action.

-- Chloe's hair expands into a catcher's mitt stopping the
flying elevator. Medusa smiles.

84.

                    MEDUSA
          Where are my manners? I forgot to
          introduce my entourage - The
          Fashionasties! Come-come!

-- The Fashionasties burst upon the scene, guns BLAZING.
Francesca's mouth guard spits out. She melts bullets on
contact.

-- Max and Tania rush to Drusilla. Tania FIRES her "naillets"
at a hanging banner. It falls from the ceiling, flying
underneath Drusilla, creating a slide into the fountain.

-- Max starts to rush to her, but is blocked by Medusa.

                    MEDUSA
          Hello, Max. I always despised the
          way you thought you were smarter
          than everyone else.

                    MAX
          That's because I am.

                    TANIA
          Go inviso, girl!

                    MAX
          Not here!

Medusa smiles, then FIRES Her eyes at Max turning her to
stone. Tania fires her "naillets." Medusa's snakes bat them
away easily.

Tania runs behind a column. She sees Francesca continuing to
fight off the Fashionasties.

-- Marcellas spots a Member's Only Jacket in a store window.
Brings out a rocket launcher. And FIRES.

-- White hair rushes out and stops the rocket. Chloe's hair
holds it in place while she stares down Marcellas.

                    CHLOE
          Keep the Member's Only Jacket in
          the 80's.

                    MARCELLAS
          Eighties fashion is on the rise.

                    CHLOE
          I want a bob. Ain't gonna happen.
          Oh yes it can. See?

Chloe's hair suddenly turns into a bob, releasing the rocket.

                    CHLOE
          Uh oh.

The rocket flies into the store causing it to EXPLODE.

                    FRANCESCA
          I hate her.

                    MEDUSA (O.S.)
          Ahem.

Tania whips around. BLAST! Medusa turns her to stone.

Medusa turns the crowd to stone. Drusilla, the TV Host, teen
girls, boys, shoppers of all ages.

Sam tries to snap off more photos.

                    SAM
          I got a great one of Medusa!
          Noelle? Noelle?

He turns. Noelle's been turned to stone.

Francesca fights off the Fashionasties. She's becoming
visibly tired.

                    FRANCESCA
          Streak!

Chloe looks around. Marcellas exits the store wearing a
Member's Only Jacket. Medusa leers at Chloe.

                    MEDUSA
          Go on, Chloe. Help her. Or maybe
          deep down you don't want to.

Francesca continues fighting.

                    CHLOE
          Tesa, let me help you.

                    MEDUSA
          I'm sorry I have a live Twitter
          Q&A. Or is it a wax? Or a Snap
          Story.

                    CHLOE
          Wow. Am I that shallow?

Medusa FIRES her beam at Chloe. Her hair forms a tent around
her causing the beam to bounce off and hit Francesca and Sam.

86.

Chloe looks around. Scared. Her hair forms helicopter propellers and lifts off.

CRASH!

Shattered glass lands around Medusa's feet. She flies away.

EXT. PARK - DUSK

Chloe sits on a bench. Her glasses are off and her eyes are red from crying. Sirens blare in the distance.

                    LITTLE GIRL
          Hi.

Chloe's hair wipes her tears.

                    CHLOE
          Hello.

She is owner of the cat Chloe rescued earlier. She joins her on the bench.

                    LITTLE GIRL
          I'm Nicole. Remember me?

Chloe searches...

                    NICOLE
          You saved Mittens - my cat.

Chloe manages a smile. Police cars fly by.

                    CHLOE
          Now I remember.

                    LITTLE GIRL
          What's wrong?

                    CHLOE
          You wouldn't understand.

                    LITTLE GIRL
          Um, Medusa turned everyone to stone
          in the mall and you're sitting here?

Chloe turns to her.

                    LITTLE GIRL
          I saw it on TV. I wanted to go, but
          my mom had to work.

                    CHLOE
          I ran away.

                    LITTLE GIRL
          She looked scary. I'm sure your
          friends will understand.

                    CHLOE
          My friends? I let them down.

                    LITTLE GIRL
          Friends understand.

                    CHLOE
          They do?

                    LITTLE GIRL
          Uh huh. My friends do anyway. You
          just have to say you're sorry.
          Candy usually works, too.

Chloe thinks. Gets an idea. Stands.

                    LITTLE GIRL
          Where are you going?

She stands up.

                    CHLOE
          I'm going to help my friends.

                    LITTLE GIRL
          Can I make one suggestion?

                    CHLOE
          Sure.

                    LITTLE GIRL
          If you're going to be role models
          you need real superhero costumes.
          Fighting crime in mini skirts and
          stilettos is pretty impractical.
          And our moms would never let us
          wear that on Halloween. Well, maybe
          some would, but my mom doesn't let
          me play with their daughters.

Chloe smiles. Her hair extends, forming a sail. The wind
picks up, causing Chloe to float into the air.

EXT. SKY - DUSK

Chloe sails over the desert... searching. She spots what she's looking for - Van Swoon Labs.

EXT. VAN SWOON LABS - MOMENTS LATER

WHITE HAIR ROCKETS forward to an entrance door... GRIPS the door handles... *RIIIIIPS* the door off its hinges.

> CHLOE
> And no split ends, ladies.

INT. VAN SWOON LABS - CORRIDOR - CONTINUOUS

Abandoned. Chloe steals inside, works her way alongside a wall. Chloe pushes the buttons to the elevator. Buttons fly by as the elevator comes to her level. Doors open. She runs in.

Something small and in the shadows follows Chloe. Every time she takes a step, its steel leg CLICKS against the steel floor.

INT. ELEVATOR - CONTINUOUS

Chloe looks; pushes the basement button. A screen above the panel flashes, "RESTRICTED AREA. ACCESS DENIED." Chloe pushes again. The screen flashes the same message. She thinks.

> CUT TO:

EXT. ELEVATOR - MOMENTS LATER

KA-THUNK!

The elevator floor tumbles from the bottom of the elevator down the shaft as TWO LARGE "HAIR BOOTS" RETRACT. Chloe's hair begins to LOWER her down the shaft. Chloe watches the FLOOR NUMBERS fly past. She reaches the bottom. A section of hair releases from the elevator returning to Chloe.

HER HAIR FORMS A CROWBAR and wedges itself in between the elevator doors pushing them open.

WRAMMM!

Dr. Fantanburger works alone in the lab. Crates and crates, marked *Superheroine*, line the walls from floor to ceiling.

A conveyor belt pops out lipstick, skin creme, hair color, nail polish, blush etc.

                    CHLOE
          Dr. Fantanburger?

Dr. Fantanburger whips around.

                    DR. FANTANBURGER
          Noooooooooo!

FWOOOSH!

Before Chloe can react, steel cables, resembling spider webs, BURST toward her, wrapping around her in seconds.

The spiders, from the beginning, emerge. They swarm.

Her hair forms a BUZZ SAW, freeing her. Hundreds of spiders pounce on her.

                    CHLOE
          Eww! Icky! Spiders!

CHLOE'S HAIR FORMS A GIANT FLY SWATTER and systematically bats the spiders away. More spiders shoot webs at her, covering her in the metallic substance.

The spiders tackle her. Chloe's hair expands and expands. It bursts free from the webs, sending the spiders flying into computer banks.

BLA-KOOM!

There's sizzling and sparkling.

The spiders shut down. Chloe bends over, out of breath.

                    CHLOE
          I really need a juice cleanse.

Dr. Fantanburger rushes to her...

EXT. VAN SWOON CONSTRUCTION TOWER - ROOF - NIGHT

Olga emerges from a door. Frowns.

                    OLGA
          Where is Chloe?

                    MEDUSA
          I'll get her. In time.

                              OLGA
                    I see.

Medusa extends her arms. Behind her - Francesca, Max and
Tania turned to stone. Noelle and Sam also are turned to
stone. The Fashionasties flank her. Olga smiles.

                              MEDUSA
                    I have lived up to my end of the
                    bargain. Now it's your turn.

Olga smiles again. A hand behind her back reveals that she's
holding a high-tech gun.

                              OLGA
                    And I have. What a wonderful
                    display you have put on for my
                    buyers who were very interested in
                    those four, but with you, my god
                    your value just went through the
                    roof. They want you Tesa. Just like
                    you always wanted to be wanted. You
                    are my top weapon model!

She WHIPS out the high-tech gun and points. Medusa doesn't
flinch.

                              OLGA
                    I'm sorry to turn the tables like
                    this, dear.

Medusa saunters forward.

                              MEDUSA
                    Actually, I believe it's the other
                    way around.

Olga raises an eyebrow.

                              MEDUSA
                    I wanted you distracted, dahling,
                    while my real friends, The
                    Fashionasties...

Marcellas waves.

                              MEDUSA
                    ... went trolling for your toy.

Olga's eyes widen. Medusa nods. Marcellas nods. The Hulking
Prisoner, also wearing a Member's Only Jacket, rolls out The
Transapplicator.

Olga's taken aback. Reworks her smile. Medusa gleefully approaches Olga.

> MEDUSA
> Don't go sour just yet, Olga. See you are the one who always had delusions of grandeur...
>> *(holds her fingers in quotes)*
> ... I on the other hand am just a simple gal with simple goals. Being the greatest model in the world is my goal. It always has been. And now we have a captive audience to boot.

Olga's enraged.

> OLGA
> A model? You couldn't model your way into a catalog --

BLAST!

Medusa's beam turns Olga to stone.

> MEDUSA
> And that's how you silence a critic.

INT. VAN SWOON LABS - LAB - MOMENTS LATER

Dr. Fantanburger slumps in his chair. Chloe listens.

> DR. FANTANBURGER
> I never wanted any of this. She said she wanted my creativity to bring a whole new look to cosmetics.

He looks over at the stacks and stacks of crates.

> DR. FANTANBURGER
> All she wanted were new weapons to sell to any rogue nation who would buy them.

> CHLOE
> Who is she selling that to?

Dr. Fantanburger shakes his head.

                         DR. FANTANBURGER
               I suspect the answer lies there.

He points to the classified file floating around them.

                         CHLOE
               Can't you open it?

                         DR. FANTANBURGER
               I've been denied access.

Chloe looks at it. Then notices the computer's name --
DIAGNOSTIC, INTELLIGENT, VIDEO, AUTOMATON.

                         CHLOE
               D.I.V.A... cute.

                         DR. FANTANBURGER
               Diva?

                         CHLOE
               I'm a Diva. She's one, too. We all
               speak the same language. Diva?

                         COMPUTER
               That name does not compute.

Chloe smiles at Fantanburger.

                         CHLOE
               We all play coy. Diva...
               girlfriend... I need you to open up
               that little ol' classified file.

                         COMPUTER
               Access denied.

                         CHLOE
               Aw, please?

                         COMPUTER
               Access denied.

Chloe pouts.

                         CHLOE
               Oh Emm Gee. Someone needs a little
               attitude adjustment.

Chloe's hair extends and flies out in all different
directions. Pressing this button and that button. Inserting
itself into disk drives. The computer begins to go into a
frenzy. The Classified folder EXPLODES... revealing all sorts
of equations and women's bodies.

Chloe and Fantanburger study them.

MOMENTS LATER, Chloe, on a mission, storms to the door.

                         DR. FANTANBURGER
               Wait!

Chloe spins around. He brings out a test tube filled with a
thick, glowing yellow liquid.

                         DR. FANTANBURGER
               I was only able to produce one. It may
               reverse the process.

Chloe takes it. She notices the uniforms from earlier and
other things. Goes over to them.

                         CHLOE
               What are those?

                         DR. FANTANBURGER
               Just me chasing windmills.

Chloe holds up a bracelet.

                         CHLOE
               You chase windmills with these?

Dr. Fantanburger takes it from her. Presses a button on the
inside, causing the bracelet to GLOW.

                         DR. FANTANBURGER
               This bracelet was supposed to be
               used in combat. It encodes your
               brain waves into an energy field
               which--

Chloe looks at him dumbfounded.

                         DR. FANTANBURGER
               It makes you fly.

                         CHLOE
               I'll take four.

She looks at the four combat uniforms.

                         DR. FANTANBURGER
               Those adapt to the subject's DNA--

                         CHLOE
               -- Four.

She looks over at the crates of skin creme.

                         CHLOE
              And some skin creme. Oh and one
              more thing...

She looks at the rest of the crates.

EXT. SKY - NIGHT

BOOM!

Chloe ZOOMS into the air, cradling Dr. Fantanburger in her
hair, as the lab disappears in a giant EXPLOSION.

EXT. VAN SWOON CONSTRUCTION SITE - NIGHT

Full moon. MEDUSA, glammed up, steps into the
Transapplicator. The Fashionasties look on.

                         MEDUSA
              This town is in need of an extreme
              makeover!

She grabs hold of the outer rings. A SNAKE pushes the
controls. ENERGY pulses through the Transapplicator...then
Medusa. The energy rockets away from the machine and Medusa
into the night sky.

The energy causes her eyes to pulse and glow greener than
ever. POWER BEAMS, stronger than ever, rocket out of her eyes
towards the city...

--Series of Shots--

-- PEOPLE are randomly turned to stone.

-- A DOG tries to run, but is turned to stone.

-- A BUS DRIVER is turned to stone. The bus crashes into a
fire hydrant, sending an arc of water into the air.

-- TWO SECURITY GUARDS and a GERMAN SHEPHERD run onto the
roof. Guns pulled. MEDUSA aims and turns them to stone.

EXT. SKY - NIGHT

Chloe, now dressed as Streak - skin tight white costume, new
dark glasses, hot boots and backpack - soars over Angel City.

She squints as a green energy cloud rushes toward her.

                    CHLOE
          That is not smog.

She flies higher as the cloud RUMBLES underneath her. Birds,
suddenly turned to stone, drop around her.

More birds fall. Chloe weaves in and out of them, avoiding
any collision.

EXT. VAN SWOON CONSTRUCTION SITE - NIGHT

                    MEDUSA (O.S.)
          Wakey... wakey.

Francesca, Max and Tania, now normal, slowly come to. They
are bound by high-tech shackles.

                    MEDUSA
          There you are.

                    TANIA
          Where are we?

                    MEDUSA
          You are about to witness...
                    (stands up; spreads her
                     arms)
          ... history.

She looks over at Marcellas.

                    MEDUSA
          Hit it.

Marcellas presses a button to a boombox. House music BLARES.
The Supermodels! take in what the construction site roof top
has become - an elaborate fashion runway. Off to the side is
Olga and Angel City citizens (including Drusilla, Sam,
Noelle).

The stage is surrounded by TV cameras, held by stone camera
men. Medusa, in designer clothes, prances down the stage.
Looks over her stone audience.

                    MEDUSA
          Hmm. Let me see. We have models. We
          have a supermodel. Oh we need a
          photographer.

She searches the stone group, finds Sam. She aims her BEAM at
Sam. And FIRES. Sam turns back to normal. Stumbles.

                    SAM
          Where am I?
                 (realizes)
          Holy crap! Noelle?

Medusa moves seductively to him.

                    MEDUSA
          No reporter gal pal tonight
          sweetie. Just you, me and Tom Ford.
          I want you to make sure you get all
          my good sides.
                 (stoops and whispers)
          Make sure you get all of my
          friends, too.
                 (points to her hissing
                  snakes)
          They tend to get catty. That is if
          they haven't eaten one yet. Here.

She hands him a camera.

Tania extends a nail, tries to saw through the shackle.
Francesca tries to work her mouth guard out of her mouth. Max
tries to free herself as well.

Medusa skips down the catwalk. Looks over at Marcellas.

                    MEDUSA
          Let's crush this!

Marcellas flips a switch.

EXT. ANGEL CITY - VARIOUS LOCATIONS - SAME TIME

TV's around the city, in stores, screens in a Time Square
like setting, cell phones, switch to the rooftop setting.
Spotlights dance around the stage.

EXT. VAN SWOON CONSTRUCTION SITE - SAME TIME

CLOSE ON MARCELLAS. He speaks into a mic.

                    MARCELLAS
          Ladies and gentlemen, wearing a hot
          evening number from the Tom Ford
          spring collection... the greatest
          model to have ever walked the
          earth...

Francesca frowns at this.

                    FRANCESCA
          I, Francesca am the greatest model
          to ever walk--

                    MAX
          -- Not now.

Tania manages to cut one of the cables.

                    MARCELLAS
          Her highness... Medusa!

The curtains part. She winks at Marcellas.

                    MEDUSA
          Ooh. I like the highness part.

Medusa saunters out.

                    CHLOE (O.S.)
          WAIT!

Marcellas looks up. Medusa, too. The Supermodels! look up.
Sam's mouth drops.

Chloe floats above the catwalk.

                    MEDUSA
          Who's the designer?

Chloe floats in closer.

                    CHLOE
          Tesa, don't do this. This isn't
          you. You're not a monster.

She points to Olga.

                    CHLOE
          She's the monster. We're the
          monsters. I'm the monster. I made
          you like this. And I'm sorry.

Medusa stops. Tesa starts to shine through.

                    MEDUSA
               (as Tesa)
          Chloe!?!

                    CHLOE
               (smiles)
          Tesa!

98.

The Supermodels! look on. Sam stops snapping off pics. Puts
his camera down and runs to the models. He pulls, plies,
wrestles, etc.

                    FRANCESCA
          If they kiss, I vomit. And call
          Mafia.

Chloe and Medusa near each other.

                    CHLOE
          I understand, Tesa.

                    MEDUSA
          Really?

                    CHLOE
          I didn't embrace myself and who I
          was. And if you don't embrace
          yourself you can't let others in. I
          want to let you in.

Chloe nods. Medusa's look quickly returns.

                    MEDUSA
          Maybe... Maybe... Nah!

Snakes launch from Medusa's head toward Chloe. Venom drips
from their fangs. Chloe's hair punches them away. She brings
out Dr. Fantanburger's test tube.

                    CHLOE
          I won't let you down, Tesa. You're
          my friend. They're my friends.

Sam frees Max. They work on Francesca. Tania frees herself.

                    TANIA
          Did she just say we're friends?

                    MAX
          The Transapplicator really did
          alter her.

                    MEDUSA
          I was Olga's assistant. Do you
          really think I didn't know what
          would happen. This is who I am. And
          I embrace myself, Streak!

Medusa's eyes glow. The snakes' eyes glow. A green energy
bubble forms around her. It ex... pa... nds...

KA-BOOM!

The blast sends Chloe over the edge. Dr. Fantanburger's cure
flies from her grip. It crashes to the ground.

Medusa laughs. Sam turns.

                    SAM
          No!

He frees Francesca. Max frees Tania. Max strips. Sam watches.

                    MAX
          Turn around!

Max disappears.

WHITE HAIR stretches over the edge... runs across the roof
and grabs the four by the legs.

And pulls them over the edge. The four tumble to the ground.

                    CHLOE
          Hi! Are you guys o-k-a--

                    TANIA
          This isn't the time to spell!

                    CHLOE
          Hee hee. Right. Here.

She reaches into her back pack. Brings out the bracelets.

                    CHLOE
          Take these!

                    FRANCESCA
          Real or faux?

Sam sees the ground coming up.

                    SAM
          Put them on!

The ground nears. The Supermodels! put them on.

CRASH!

Well not exactly. The Supermodels! float inches above the
ground. Thanks to the bracelets. Chloe cushions Sam's tumble
with her hair.

                    SAM
          Whoa.

100.

                    FRANCESCA
          Francesca can fly?

                    CHLOE
          That's Shimmer. And yes.

Chloe reaches into her back pack, brings out the costumes.

                    FRANCESCA
          Hmm.

                    MAX
          It won't help me.

                    CHLOE
          Dr. Fantanburger said it would
          conform to your STD. I mean DOA.

                    MAX
               (smiles)
          I know what you mean.

                    TANIA
          I won't be needing that.

                    CHLOE
          Honey, now isn't the time to
          complain.

                    TANIA
          Oh I'm not.

Tania extends her fingers... wiggles... slowly the red nail
polish begins to flow over her fingers, then her hands, up
her arms... the models look on in amazement as Tania is
completely covered head-to-toe in red nail polish, resembling
a red 'Silver Surfer."

                    CHLOE
          That is hot.

                    MAX
          Uh-huh.

KA-THUD!

The ground *TREMBLES* as Medusa lands. Her snakes have now
grown to enormous proportions. She even slithers on top of
one.

Chloe turns to the girls.

                    CHLOE
          Oh Emm Gee! What should we do?

                    MAX
          You tell us. You're top model.

Chloe smiles at this. Max smiles back. She turns toward Sam
who picks up a garbage can lid to block the Anaconda's fangs.

A confident Chloe turns to the models.

                    CHLOE
          Supermodels! Work it!

--Series of Shots--

-- Chloe springs into action... forms oversized pony tails.
Francesca and Tania leap onto her pony tails, propelling
themselves into the air.

-- Medusa launches her snakes and FIRES her beams.

-- A snake from her head EXTEEEEEEEEENDS, picks up a bus and
launches it at them. Tania's "naillets" split the bus in
half.

-- Chloe's hair rips a light pole out of the ground and bats
away more snakes and beams.

-- Francesca spins through the air firing her mouth
repeatedly, defeating one snake after another.

-- Tania springs onto a light pole, firing her nails...
pinning this snake and that one.

-- Max reaches out from a building and pulls the snakes into
it hard.

The Supermodels! close in on Medusa.

                    CHLOE
          Now!

-- Medusa's power beams rush out of her eyes. Francesca
blocks it with rays from her mouth, each pushing in the
opposite direction. Francesca strains to push hers more.

-- Chloe pulls something out from her hair. The skin creme.
Her hair unscrews it and launches it at Medusa. Then another.
And another. And another.

-- The girls cover their noses.

                    MAX
          Ugh, that stuff does stink!

The fumes begin to make Medusa dizzy. She stumbles. The
snakes drunkenly drop off her head.

-- Tania crouches and fires her nails at MEDUSA, knocking the
snakes off her head.

Chloe's hair picks up several steel beams. She flies them
toward Medusa. One lands in front of her. Then another. And
another. The beams begin to form a circular prison around
her.

                    CHLOE
          Now!

Francesca FIRES, causing the beams to melt together.

Medusa's defeated.

The Supermodels! re-group. Out of breath.

                    MAX
          Wow.

                    TANIA
          Is it really over?

Chloe nods. Francesca frowns.

                    FRANCESCA
          My mouth... my lovely mouth.

She picks up a piece of shattered mirror glass. Checks her
teeth in it.

WHAM!

The girls turn. Steel beams fly everywhere. Medusa storms
out. Her eyes glow like they've never glowed before.

                    MEDUSA
          I will destroy you. I am the
          greatest model in the world!

The girls are dumbfounded. Chloe smiles.

                    CHLOE
          Hey, Medusa. You know all this
          fighting is bad for your
          complexion. You're breaking out.

                    MEDUSA
          What!?!

Chloe spots a piece of broken glass. She walks up to her.

                    CHLOE
          Here.

Medusa snatches it from her and looks. Her face is fine.
Something suddenly grabs one her snakes.

                    MEDUSA
          What!?!

Something Invisible aims the snakes at the mirror. Medusa's
eye glow with fury and fire.

The beam bounces off the glass and back toward Medusa.

                    MEDUSA
          Noooooooooo!

Before she can finish, Medusa turns to stone. Max appears
behind her. Smiles at her friends.

EXT. ANGEL CITY - VARIOUS LOCATIONS - SAME TIME

Stone people now turn back to dazed normal ones. Olga
stumbles forward. As does Noelle, Drusilla, the TV Host and
Crazy Eight!

INT. VAN SWOON TOWERS - DAY

Olga, back in power, addresses reporters. Sam and Noelle
stand in front.

                         OLGA
              I wanted to stop her, but under
              Medusa's control there was simply
              nothing I could do.

                         NOELLE
          What about Dr. Fantanburger?

                         OLGA
              A tragedy really. He was killed in
              a mishap at one of our plants.

Olga sighs.

                         NOELLE
              Are the rumors true you had Medusa
              moved to one of your research
              facilities?

104.

                    OLGA
          Yes, I believe our medical staff
          can learn and perhaps help Miss
          Thompson overcome her tragic
          accident. Good day.

Reporters leave. Noelle turns one more time to Olga.

                    NOELLE
          What about the Supermodels?!

                    OLGA
          I'm grateful for all their help.

Noelle and Sam leave. Olga smiles...

                    OLGA
          You can come out now.

Max appears. The other girls fly in through Olga's open
window. Olga faces all four.

                    OLGA
          Quite the ensem's.

                    CHLOE
          You have a lot to answer for.

                    OLGA
          Au contraire. You destroyed my
          research facility.

                    CHLOE
          That was no research facility for
          cosmetics. I read the files. You
          were making us into weapons.

                    OLGA
          And so I have.

                    TANIA
          The commercial?

                    OLGA
          A demo for our buyers abroad.

Chloe steps forward.

                    CHLOE
          You had no right to take Tesa.

Olga smiles again. She clearly has the upper hand.

                    OLGA
          Oh my dear. I have every right...

She turns to them.

                    OLGA
          I'm her mother. But let us not be
          enemies. Let us be partners.
          Imagine the possibilities.

Silence. Chloe steps forward.

                    CHLOE
          We're going to keep our eye on you.
          You wanted Superheroines.

                    MAX
          Now you have them.

They fly away. Olga SLAMS her fist on the table.

INT. DAILY HERALD - MR. BLAKE'S OFFICE - DAY (MORNING)

A beaming Mr. Blake welcomes Noelle and Sam with open arms.

                    MR. BLAKE
          There they are! My heroes!

Noelle smiles as Mr. Blake circles them, sniffing the air.

                    MR. BLAKE
          What's that I smell? Oh Pulitzer!

Sam shifts. Noelle takes in the accolades.

                    MR. BLAKE
          Let me see the pics. Gimme, gimme,
          gimme.

Sam shifts again. His dad notices.

                    SAM
          Dad...

                    MR. BLAKE
          You have the pics right?

                    SAM
          Yeah.

                    MR. BLAKE
          Well...

                    SAM
          I can't show them.

It's like a truck ran over Noelle and Mr. Blake, who smiles.

                    MR. BLAKE
          Why?

                    SAM
          The Van Swoon girls aren't the
          Supermodels!

Mr. Blake's eyes blink rapidly.

                    MR. BLAKE
          No pics?

                    SAM
          No, Dad.

                    MR. BLAKE
          Don't call me DAD! Out! Get out!

Mr. Blake shows them the door.

EXT. STREET - DAY (MORNING)

Noelle slaps Sam across the arm as they walk down the street.

                    NOELLE
          I've never been fired.

                    SAM
          We're a team! There's not a paper
          in town that won't want us.

                    NOELLE
               (yells)
          There's only one paper!

People look up. Sam and Noelle crane their necks. The
Supermodels! dart across the sky.

                    NOELLE
          I know it's them.

                    SAM
          Think again.

Sam points. Noelle's mouth drops. Chloe, Francesca, Max and
Tania walk down the street carrying shopping bags. Chloe
stops.

>   CHLOE
>   Sam, right?

>   SAM
>   Right!

>   CHLOE
>   You guys, this is the photographer
>   that I was telling you about. His
>   pics crush anything Nigel ever did.

Francesca lays an arm around Sam.

>   FRANCESCA
>   Francesca will call you for
>   headshots.

>   SAM
>   Yes, yes.

Chloe gives Sam a card.

>   CHLOE
>   Here's my number. Call me.

She gives Sam a peck on the cheek. As do the other girls.
They keep walking. Noelle, mouth agape, tries to understand
and take it all in.

As Chloe and the girls continue to walk, Max taps her
bluetooth.

>   MAX
>   The holograms work just fine, Dr.
>   Fantanburger.

INT. CHLOE'S FIRST APARTMENT - SAME TIME

Has now been converted into a high-tech lab. Dr. Fantanburger
smiles into his microphone.

>   DR. FANTANBURGER
>   Excellent. Diva and I will continue
>   to perfect them.

>   COMPUTER/DIVA
>   You got that right, Fanty.

*Fantanburger's computer now speaks with the sass of a gay
black man.*

                    DR. FANTANBURGER
          I need to work on your programming
          some more. That explosion must've
          damaged some circuits.

                    DIVA
          All right but be careful where
          those fingers go roaming.

INT. CHLOE'S CONDO - LATER

Chloe's on her iPhone, while the TV plays in the background.
She adds Max, Francesca and Tania to her friends on Facebook.

Max, now clearly her roommate, speaks on the phone.

                    MAX
          Yes, Mom I know it's a red carpet
          event. I am wearing underwear. No I
          won't go with Crazy Eight.

She looks down at the cover. The Supermodels! are on it.

Chloe looks up at the TV. MAYOR DINES, 50s, portly, addresses
reporters.

                    MAYOR
          Now with Medusa out of the picture,
          The Supermodels! have now turned
          their attention to the growing
          crime rate in Angel City.

EXT. CITY HALL - SAME TIME

Noelle raises her hand... beating Katie Ward.

                    NOELLE
          How will they know if we need them?

The Mayor smiles.

                    MAYOR
          They gave us a signal.

He approaches a console. Flips a switch.

BOOM! BOOM! CRACKLE! BOOM!

Firecrackers launch into the sky. They form...

A CAMERA. The Camera flashes.

Below on a billboard, stand Chloe, Francesca, Max and Tania
in heroic poses. Chloe smiles. We realize they're not photos.
They're the real things.

                         CHLOE
               Supermodels! Work it!

The four fly off the edge of the building. Ready to fight a
supervillain somewhere...

                                        FLASH TO BLACK.

ABOUT THE SCREENWRITER

Author photograph by NJ Bourque

Colin Costello is a screenwriter, director, journalist and comic book geek. His feature films include, *The Stream* (2013) and *Traveling Without Moving* (2017). His award-winning short films include two DC Comics Fan Films, *Committed* (2016) and *Little Man of Steel* (2012), the horror short, *Realitory: Welcome to The Machine* (2012) and *First Kiss* (2008). He has also written for the Emmy-nominated educational TV series, *Moochie-Kalala Detective's Club*. He resides in Los Angeles, CA.

120pages

EXPOSURE. CREDIBILITY. PROFIT.

PUBLISH YOUR SCREENPLAY WITH **120pages**!

You've spent countless hours — maybe years — writing your screenplay. You believe it in it, but it has not yet been picked up for production.

By publishing your screenplay with 120pages, you will:

- Earn income from your work
- Give your screenplay exposure
- Build your credibility as a screenwriter

Visit **120pages.com** today to learn more!